W9-BOO-824
3 1265 01321 1265

THE CAT SITTER'S PAJAMAS

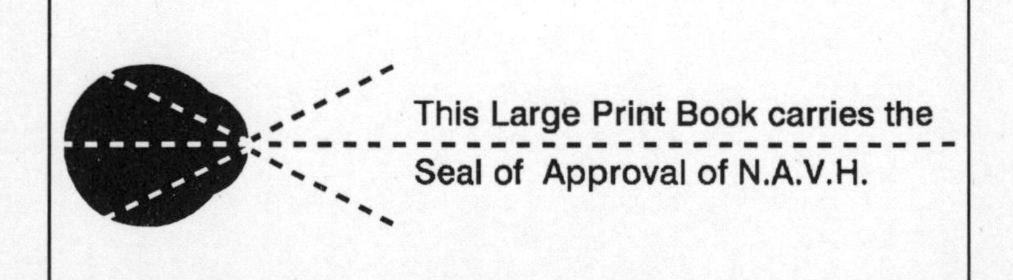
This Large Print Book carries the
Seal of Approval of N.A.V.H.

A DIXIE HEMINGWAY MYSTERY

THE CAT SITTER'S PAJAMAS

BLAIZE CLEMENT

THORNDIKE PRESS
A part of Gale, Cengage Learning

Detroit • New York • San Francisco • New Haven, Conn • Waterville, Maine • London

A Dixie Hemingway Mystery.
Thorndike Press, a part of Gale, Cengage Learning.

Thorndike Press® Large Print Mystery.
The text of this Large Print edition is unabridged.
Other aspects of the book may vary from the original edition.
Set in 16 pt. Plantin.

LIBRARY OF CONGRESS CATALOGING-IN-PUBLICATION DATA

Clement, Blaize.
The cat sitter's pajamas / by Blaize Clement.
pages ; cm. — (Thorndike Press large print mystery)
ISBN 978-1-4104-4642-8 (hardcover) — ISBN 1-4104-4642-5 (hardcover)
1. Hemingway, Dixie (Fictitious character)—Fiction. 2. Women detectives—Florida—Fiction. 3. Cats—Fiction. 4. Sarasota (Fla.)—Fiction. 5. Large type books. I. Title.
PS3603.L463C44 2012b
813'.6—dc23 2011051824

Published in 2012 by arrangement with St. Martin's Press, LLC.

Printed in the United States of America
1 2 3 4 5 6 7 16 15 14 13 12

This book is dedicated to my family, always loyal, always supportive, always *there* for me whenever I need them. I hope they know that even when I neglect to tell them, my love surrounds each of them every moment.

ACKNOWLEDGMENTS

As usual, this book and all the books in the Dixie Hemingway Mystery Series owe their existence to the very capable hands of Marcia Markland, Senior Editor at St. Martin's/Thomas Dunne Books, and to Assistant Editor Kat Brzozowski.

Copy Editor India Cooper's eagle eye caught authorial goofs such as having a lane curve in a particular direction, except when it didn't. Thanks, India!

No book finds a reader unless readers know it's out there. Hector DeJean, Associate Publicity Director, and Sarah Melnyk, Publicity Manager, are tireless in letting people looking for their latest "Dixie fix" know when it's on its way to them.

During the creation of the book, the "Thursday Group" — Greg Jorgensen, Madeline Mora-Sumonte, Jane Phelan, and Linda Bailey — patiently listened to half-baked ideas and tentative explorations.

Thanks, guys!

A million thanks to the distribution reps who see that bookstores have the books, and the overworked and underpaid booksellers who loyally display, recommend, and promote Dixie Hemingway. And to Al Zuckerman at Writer's House, the consummate gentleman who has introduced some of the world's greatest writers to the world, but still pays me as much attention as he does them. That's a rare quality in an agent, and I value it highly.

When I need answers to sticky questions relating to local law enforcement rules, I turn to homicide detective Chris Iorio of the Sarasota County Sheriff's Department, who always patiently answers my law enforcement questions.

Last but by no means least, a big thank you to all the deputies who keep Siesta Key its calm, laid-back self. You may not realize it, but everybody on the Key recognizes your work and is grateful for it.

How dreary to be somebody!
How public, like a frog
To tell your name the livelong day
To an admiring bog!
— Emily Dickinson (1830–1886)

1

When you live in a resort area, every third person you meet on the street may be somebody famous. Here in Sarasota, which probably has more famous personalities per capita than any other city in the world, you might sit beside Toby and Itzhak Perlman in a movie theater or see Stephen King in Circle Books on St. Armands Key. We locals stay cool about it. We don't run up to them and gush like yokels. We just dip our heads in silent respect and hope they notice how generous we are to grant them privacy. If we should become friends with one of them, the way I did with Cupcake Trillin and his wife, Jancey, we don't go around bragging about it. We treat them like any other friend, but we're always aware that fate has given them an extra allotment of talent or looks or determination that the rest of us don't have.

I'm Dixie Hemingway, no relation to you-know-who, that other famous Floridian. I live on Siesta Key, which is one of the semitropical barrier islands off Sarasota — the others being Casey, Bird, Lido, St. Armands, and Longboat. Connected by two drawbridges, Siesta is the closest to the mainland, and in most respects, it's like a small town. People gather for sand-sculpting contests, Fourth of July fireworks, and Christmas tree lighting. They run with their dogs on the beach, walk to the post office inside Davidson Drugs, gossip over coffee at one of our gourmet coffee shops. So far, we've been able to keep chain stores off the island, and we're proud that all our businesses are locally owned. Except in "season," when snowbirds come, the key is home to about seven thousand people. During season, we swell to about twenty-four thousand, and traffic and tempers get a little quicker.

I live here for the same reason so many famous people have second or third or maybe eighth homes here — because it's a paradise of riotous colors, balmy sea breezes, cool talcum sand beaches, and every songbird and seabird you can think of. Snowy egrets walk around in our parking lots, great blue herons stand vigil on people's lawns, and if we look up we see the silhouette of frigate birds flying above the clouds like ships without a home.

My only claims to fame are that once I went totally bonkers while TV cameras rolled, and later I killed a man. I was a sheriff's deputy when I went crazy, but I didn't kill anybody until after I'd got myself more or less together and became a pet sitter. Pet sitting is a lot more dangerous than people think.

Cupcake Trillin's fame came from being an immovable inside linebacker for the Tampa Bay Buccaneers. He's the size of a walk-in closet and has one of the tenderest hearts in the universe. He and I became friends when we rescued the baby of his best friend.

He and Jancey had left their two cats, Elvis and Lucy, in my care while they spent a two-week vacation in Parma, Italy. For Jancey, it was a long-planned chance to learn to make authentic Italian dishes. For Cupcake, it was a last-minute change of plans — he'd been widely reported to be attending a private meeting of fellow athletes who sponsored a camp for disadvantaged kids — but a welcome opportunity to get personal with honest-to-God prosciutto and Parmesan cheese.

The Trillins lived on the south end of the

Key in an exclusive gated community called Hidden Shores. Since the famous and rich are always on guard against intruders, the main difference between Hidden Shores and a maximum security prison is that it costs big bucks to be confined in Hidden Shores. In addition to a security gate, a tall stucco wall hung with riotous bougainvillea and trumpet vine surrounds the area. Those pretty flowers conceal coiled razor ribbon.

Cupcake and Jancey had been in Italy a week on the Tuesday morning when their lives and mine took a sudden turn. It was early, with a few horsetail clouds fanning a mango sky, when I drove up to the Hidden Shores gatehouse. I punched in my temporary security code and watched the gate slide open. In our humid climate, most entry gates are built of aluminum, but this one had been powder coated to look like wrought iron. A good seven feet tall, it had sharp spikes at the top to discourage anybody rash enough to think about climbing it. As it opened, I kept one eye on the rearview mirror in case a robber or serial killer tried to whip around my Bronco and race through ahead of me — places like Hidden Shores are guaranteed to make anybody paranoid.

A human is usually at the gate, but at that

hour the gate was unmanned. I guess the security people figure robbers work nine to five. As I pulled through the opened gate, my name, the time, and the date were electronically recorded at a security company's office. More than likely, my photo had also been snapped by a hidden camera.

In the Trillins' driveway, I took a moment to flip open my notebook to remind myself of my temporary house code number, then hustled up the path to the front door. I was humming under my breath when I punched in my code. I think I was still humming when I turned the doorknob and pushed the door open, but the instant I stepped into the foyer I froze.

Houses have signature odors as distinctive as a human's individual scent. I couldn't have accurately described the unique breath of the Trillins' house, but I knew it well enough to detect a change in it.

At about the same instant I realized an intruder was in the house, a willowy woman with skim-milky skin stepped from the living room into the foyer. Her long titian hair was lit by subtle hues that only occur on very small children and women with expensive colorists. She wore bright scarlet lipstick, and her fingernails and toenails were the same bright red. Except for an oversized, brightly printed man's shirt hanging unbuttoned from her narrow shoulders, she was naked.

I tried not to look, but it's not every day you run into a naked woman with a Brazilian wax job in the shape of a valentine heart. The pubic heart was red like her hair, which made the old naughty doggerel run through my head: *Mix another batch and dye your snatch to match!*

She gave me a gracious, hostessy smile and extended a limp hand as if she expected me to cross the foyer and shake it.

In a husky, seductive voice, she said, "I'm Briana."

Under the terms of my contract with my clients, I make it clear that I need the names of all the people who have permission to come in while they're gone. Otherwise, if I find anybody in the house, I'll take them as unlawful intruders and act accordingly.

I said, "I can't let you stay here without the owner's permission."

Her smile grew more serene. "You don't understand. I'm Cupcake's wife."

I said, "That will come as a surprise to the wife with him right now."

Her eyes clouded in momentary confusion. "Excuse me?"

My throat tightened. The woman seemed

to really believe what she'd said.

From somewhere in the house, a faint noise sounded — the *click* a refrigerator door makes when it's surreptitiously closed, maybe, or the *snick!* from unlocking a glass slider to a lanai.

Without another word, I stepped backward and pulled the door shut behind me. Outside, I took out my cell phone to call the cops, and then hesitated. Ordinary people can have intruders in their house and it never makes the papers. Cupcake was famous, and reporters would salivate at a report of a naked woman in his house while he and his wife were away.

Instead of dialing 911, I called Cupcake.

Cupcake answered with a note of concern in his voice. "Dixie?"

For some reason, I was surprised that caller ID worked all the way across the Atlantic.

I said, "There's a woman in your house. She says her name is Briana. I think somebody else may be in there, too."

Cupcake said, "Oh, *ma-a-a-an.*"

He sounded like a kid learning his ball game has been called off.

He lowered the phone to yell at his wife. "Jancey, it's Dixie. There's another woman. This one broke into the house."

Jancey took the phone. "She's in our *house?*"

I said, "I'm afraid so."

Cupcake said something too muffled for me to hear, and Jancey quit talking to me to talk to him.

"Are you kidding me? She's in our *house,* Cupcake! In our shower! Sleeping in our bed! And you want to *protect* her?"

I grinned. Cupcake's tender heart sometimes forces Jancey to play the heavy.

There were some more muffled sounds, probably Cupcake wresting the phone from her.

He said, "Those women that stalk us have to be some kind of sick. I feel sorry for them."

Jancey yelled, "They stalk Cupcake, not me!"

Cupcake sighed. "Call the police, but try to get them to commit her or put her in a hospital or something."

I said, "She acted like she knew you. Do you know anybody named Briana?"

"Never heard of her."

Jancey got on the phone again. "Dixie, get that woman out of my house. Are the cats okay?"

"I haven't seen them yet. I came outside to call you as soon as she told me she was

Cupcake's wife."

"She said *what?* Oh my God!"

I could have slapped myself for telling her that. What woman wants to hear that another woman is going around claiming her husband? But it was done, and I couldn't take it back. At least I hadn't told about the woman being naked, or about the huge shirt she'd worn. I was pretty sure the shirt was one of Cupcake's.

I hurried to tell Jancey I would have the woman taken away, got off the line, and called 911.

"I'm a pet sitter, and I just walked in on an intruder in a client's house. A woman. She seemed mentally disturbed and should be handled with care. There may be another person in the house as well."

I gave the address, but when the dispatcher asked for the homeowner's name, I tried to distract her.

"It's a gated community. Whoever comes will have to use a code to get in. I guess they could use mine."

Crisply, the dispatcher said, "No problem, ma'am. We have our own code. A deputy will be there shortly."

I grinned and shut off the phone. I knew about the bar code affixed to the side of every Sarasota County emergency and law enforcement vehicle. As the vehicle approaches the gate, an electronic reader scans the code and automatically opens the gate.

I also knew that reporters with police scanners listened to 911 calls. I doubted that any of them knew Cupcake's address, and I didn't think they'd go to the effort of looking up the address I'd given the dispatcher. At least I hoped they wouldn't. I hoped they'd yawn and wait for something juicier than a cat sitter calling about an intruder. If the stars were in the right alignment for Cupcake, the woman in his house would be hustled off without the world ever knowing she'd been there.

I waited in the Bronco, imagining Briana inside the house wondering why I was still there. Or maybe she wasn't. She had seemed so spaced out that she might have forgotten me as soon as I left. Cupcake was right, the woman was mentally ill. Jancey was probably right, too. The woman had probably been in their bed and in their shower.

Deputy Jesse Morgan and an unsworn female deputy from the Community Policing unit arrived in separate cars, both parking behind me in the driveway and walking toward me with the near swagger that uniforms give both men and women. I didn't know the woman, but Morgan and I had met a few times in situations I didn't want to remember. I was never sure if he thought I was a total kook or if he thought I just had really bad luck.

Morgan is one of Siesta Key's sworn deputies, meaning he carries a gun. He's lean, with sharp cheekbones and knuckles, and hair trimmed so short as to be almost nonexistent. He wears dark mirrored shades that hide any emotion in his eyes, but one ear sports a small diamond stud. I'm not sure what that diamond says, but it's about the only thing about Morgan that indicates a personal life outside the sheriff's department. The Key has so little true crime that most of our law enforcement is done by the unsworn deputies of the Community Policing unit, like the woman with him. Community Police officers wear dark green shorts and white knit shirts. Except for a gun, their belts bristle with the same equipment used by the sworn deputies.

Morgan greeted me with the halfhearted enthusiasm with which a dog greets a vet wearing rubber gloves and holding a syringe. Civil, but pretty sure he's not going to like what's coming. He introduced Deputy Clara Beene, and she and I did a brief handshake. Beene seemed more intrigued by the house and grounds than by me, so I figured she had never heard of me. Like I said, my fame is very limited.

I said, "I'm taking care of two cats that live here. When I went in, I found a woman in the house. She claimed to be the wife of the owner, but I know she's not. I think somebody else was in there, too. I came out and called the owners. They don't know who the woman is. They think she must be mentally disturbed, and they asked for her to be committed to a hospital or something instead of put in jail."

Morgan tilted his head to peer down at me. If I'd been able to see his eyes, I imagine they would have had a sharp glint in them. We both knew how hard it is for law enforcement officers to do anything constructive about lawbreakers who are mentally ill. Under Florida law, a cop who believes a person is about to commit suicide or kill somebody can initiate the Baker Act that involuntarily commits a person for testing. The commitment period lasts only seventy-two hours, and unless two psychiatrists petition the court to extend the commitment time for involuntary treatment, the person is released.

I doubted that Briana would be considered an imminent threat to herself or anybody else. More likely, she would be considered an extreme neurotic with a delusional crush on a famous athlete.

Without commenting on what he thought about trying to get Briana hospitalized, Morgan flipped open his notebook and clicked his pen. "What made you think somebody else was in the house with the woman?"

"Just a noise I heard. Like maybe somebody unlocking the lanai slider. It could have been something else."

"But you didn't see anybody else."

"No, it was just a little clicking noise."

"What's the homeowner's name?"

"Trillin."

He lowered his pen and angled his head at me. "*Cupcake* Trillin?"

"I hope we can keep this out of the news."

His jawbone jutted out a bit, like he'd just bit down hard on his back teeth. "I'll just put 'Trillin' as the owner's name. You ever see the woman inside before?"

"No. She said her name was Briana."

"Briana who?"

Beene, the Community Policing woman, said, "She just goes by Briana. That one name. She's a famous model."

Morgan and I turned to look at her, and she shrugged. "I watch *Entertainment Tonight.*"

Morgan's nostrils flared slightly as if it might be against department policy to watch shows like that.

"So?"

"So she's here in Sarasota. I heard it on the news."

Beene looked from Morgan to me. "You must have heard of her. She was all over the news last year. You know, she's the model that caused a big stink at the fashion show in Milan."

Morgan and I shook our heads. I might have heard about somebody in a cat show who'd made the news, but fashion shows were out of my world.

As if he had heard all he could stand about fashion models, Morgan put his pen and pad away and took a deep breath. With Beene a step behind him, he strode manfully to the door and rapped on it.

He yelled, "Sarasota Sheriff's Department!"

The door didn't open. No sound came from inside.

Morgan waited a few seconds, then knocked and shouted again. Nobody answered.

I felt a little shiver of guilty relief. Briana and whoever had been in the house with her had probably slipped out the back door while I watched the front. Maybe they were halfway to Tampa by now. Maybe they would never come back. Maybe Briana had learned her lesson and would stop stalking Cupcake.

Morgan turned to look at me as if it were my fault nobody had answered the door. "You got a key?"

"I have a security code."

"Please use it."

Feeling important under their gaze, I stepped forward and punched in my special number. The lock clicked, and I turned the knob and opened the door. Morgan motioned me aside, and he and Beene went into the house.

Once again, intuition or subliminal cues made the hairs on the back of my neck stand up, as if trouble was barreling toward me.

I said, "Don't let the cats out."

My sixth sense was right about trouble coming, but it wasn't two runaway cats.

2

Morgan and Beene left the foyer and went into the living room.

From where I stood by the front door, I couldn't see them, but I heard Beene say, "Uh-oh," the way people do when they see something bad.

Morgan didn't answer.

Beene didn't say anything else.

Nobody said anything else. Something was wrong.

I inched forward and tried to peer around the edge of the archway into the living room. All I could see was Morgan's back where he had squatted on the floor to examine something. I became aware of an off-putting scent reminiscent of floral tributes leaning on a casket, that frigid, artificial, cloying fragrance you never forget. It's also the odor of death.

A movement on the floor near Morgan caught my eye, a slow oozing, a snail's trail of dark red, a glutinous horror inching across the floor. Dead bodies don't bleed, and this blood was moving so slowly it could have come from a dying body or one whose death was only minutes old. I stepped backward, out of the foyer and into fresh air.

After a minute or two, the deputies came outside, Beene pale and pink-eyed and walking face forward, Morgan backing out behind her with a phone to his ear.

Morgan gave the address and said, "We've got a Signal Five here. Adult female. Killer suspect possibly still inside. We need backup."

Signal Five is code for a murdered body. He didn't say by what means the body had been killed, but the blood I'd seen told me it wasn't by poison or suffocation.

Officer Beene and I made eye contact, and for a moment we stared at each other in silent sadness for a life that had been violently ended. Then she turned to go about her official duties, and I was left to deal with guilt and doubt dancing around me like dark sprites. The sound I'd heard must have been the killer coming into the house. Maybe Briana hadn't heard the sound I'd heard, maybe I should have warned her, maybe I had wasted too much time calling Cupcake and Jancey before I called 911. I imagined somebody slipping into the house behind Briana and killing her while I sat unknowing in the driveway.

Morgan snapped his phone closed and turned to me. "Don't leave. You'll have to talk to Homicide."

As usual, his dark shades hid the expression in his eyes, but his voice bore the custard skin of pity.

My face grew hot, and I folded my arms over my chest. "I know."

Not so long ago, when somebody in the sheriff's department said the word "homicide," chances were they'd meant Homicide Detective J. P. Guidry, known to his friends and colleagues as Guidry, known to his mother as Jean Pierre, known to me as the second man I'd loved in all my life. But Guidry had returned to New Orleans several months ago. I could have gone with him. He had wanted me to go with him. *I* had wanted to go with him, but I had spent over three years learning to live again after my husband and little girl had been killed in a senseless accident, and I'd still been emotionally squishy, afraid I'd lose myself if I left the surf and sea breezes that had sustained me all my life.

Like everybody else in the sheriff's department, Morgan had known that Guidry and I were *together,* emotionally and physically and every other way. But Guidry and I were both intensely private people, and when he left we didn't announce to the world why I didn't go with him. Some people probably believed he had chosen to leave me behind and felt sorry for me. Others may have guessed it had been my choice not to go and pitied me for being so stupid. I didn't know what Morgan thought, but he had other reasons to think I was jinxed, so he probably felt sorry for me just on general principle.

Forcing my voice to sound neutral, I said, "You have a new homicide guy?"

Morgan shook his head. "Not yet. Hard to get somebody as good as Guidry."

That was for damn sure.

Inclining my head toward the house, I said, "After I saw the woman and exited the premises, I was out here the entire time. I didn't hear a gunshot."

He said, "Ummm." His face was so neutral he could have stood in a department store window and people would have believed he was a mannequin.

My face flamed again and I pressed my lips together. I had seen the blood, and Morgan had given a murder code, not a suicide code. So Briana had been either shot or cut. But I was a former deputy, and I knew better than to ask Morgan which it had been. In the first place, the department wouldn't give any information until after the medical examiner had signed off on the body. In the second place, my presence would automatically make me one of the suspects.

Morgan and Beene strode down a walk leading to the back of the house, probably looking for signs of forcible entry. I walked to my Bronco and leaned on the back bumper. I pulled out my cell phone and called Cupcake again.

He answered on the first ring. "Dixie, did they get her out?"

I cleared my throat. "Cupcake, I hate to tell you this, but the woman is dead."

"What do you mean, dead?"

"I mean *dead* dead, as in no longer living. While I called you and nine-one-one and waited for the deputies to get here, somebody came in and killed her."

A beat or two went by. "Dixie, if this is a joke, it's not funny."

I heard Jancey in the distance. "Is that Dixie? Did she get rid of that woman?"

I said, "It's no joke, Cupcake. I thought somebody was in the house with her because

I heard a noise, but what I heard must have been a killer entering the house. I'm here with a couple of deputies waiting for the crime-scene people. I imagine I'll be one of the suspects."

"Good God, Dixie, why would they suspect you?"

"Because I was here."

He heaved a great sigh, as if I had just confirmed some awful suspicion he'd long held. "Are the cats okay?"

"I don't know yet. I didn't see them, but they're probably hiding. I won't know anything until the crime-scene investigators get here."

"I think we'd better come home now."

"Probably."

We promised each other we'd stay in touch, and I turned off my phone.

Cupcake wanted to come home because he was concerned about his cats and his house, and because he was creeped out at learning that a woman who'd been stalking him had been murdered. He didn't realize yet that he would also be on a list of suspects. Criminal investigators know that most murders are personal, so if a stalker gets murdered in the home of a famous person, that famous person is going to be suspected of having something to do with it even if he was in another country when the murder took place.

Morgan and Beene were still investigating the back and sides of the house when several vehicles pulled into the driveway behind my Bronco. An ambulance with two EMTs, an unmarked officer's car driven by Sergeant Woodrow Owens, and a green and white deputy's vehicle with two deputies I didn't know. I straightened up when I saw Sergeant Owens. Owens is a tall, lanky African American with basset eyes and a slow drawl that masks one of the quickest minds in the universe. I was in his unit when I was a deputy, so standing up straight was an instinctive reflex because Owens didn't brook any lazy-ass slouching. He had also been the officer who had come in person to tell me my husband and little girl were dead. I hadn't stood up straight then, but buckled like a felled tree. Owens had held me tenderly as a mother.

He said, "Dixie? What's the story?"

"I'm cat sitting for Mr. and Mrs. Trillin."

Before he could ask what I knew he would ask, I said, "Yes, that's Cupcake Trillin. His wife is Jancey Trillin. They're in Italy. I went inside the house and found a woman named Briana in there. She claimed to be Cupcake's wife, but I knew that wasn't true, and she seemed mentally unhinged, so I came outside and called Cupcake to make sure she didn't have permission to be in his house. He said he'd never heard of her, so I called nine-one-one, and Deputy Morgan came with another deputy named Beene from Community Policing. They went inside and found the woman dead. I saw blood, so she was either shot or stabbed. I didn't hear a gunshot while I waited."

"Where are the deputies now?"

Just as he asked, Morgan and Beene rounded the far corner of the house. When they saw the cars and officers, they broke into a trot and joined me and Owens.

Morgan said, "We checked all the outside doors and windows. Didn't see any sign of forcible entry."

Owens turned to the gathered deputies and EMTs and tilted his head toward the house. "Let's go in."

I said, "Don't let the cats out."

Every head turned to give me an incredulous gape.

I shrugged. "Sorry, but my job is to take care of the two cats in the house. If you'd like, I can take them to a boarding place so they won't be in your way."

They all exchanged looks, imagining going about their jobs while two cats climbed over a dead body and tracked through blood.

Owens said, "Okay, come in and get them."

I said, "I'll get carrying cases," and loped off to the Bronco for two folding cardboard cat carriers.

The officers waited until I was in line, then moved forward with Owens in the lead. He and the EMTs went straight to the woman's body, while the other deputies fanned out to search the house. I pretended to look for cats behind the sofas and chairs, but I was pretty sure that I would find Elvis and Lucy in the media room in their overhead runway or at the top of their fancy climbing tree. If they'd been scared by strangers in the house, they would have climbed the tree for safety. If they hadn't even known strangers were there, they would be up the tree anyway because it was their favorite place.

Owens stood up from his stooped position over the woman's body. "Dixie, can you identify her?"

"I've only seen her once."

"That's more than anybody else has seen her. Just take a look and tell us if she's the same woman who introduced herself as . . . what did you say her name was?"

"Briana. Officer Beene has heard of her. She's a famous model, just uses the one name."

"Okay, is this dead woman the same woman who said her name was Briana?"

The EMTs stood up and backed away so I could get a clear view, and I crossed the room. Suddenly shy in the presence of death, I looked at the body before I looked at her face. Something seemed wrong. The woman had a stocky build, for one thing, not long and limber the way Briana had been. She was no longer nude under a big printed shirt but wore utilitarian khaki slacks and a bloodstained white shirt. She wore shoes as well, sensible low-heeled and laced-up leather. Not the kind of clothes I expected a famous model to wear. When I let my gaze travel upward, I saw dark, short-cropped hair. I did not allow myself to linger over the grinning slit in the woman's throat.

I felt off balance, as if somebody was playing a trick on me.

I said, "That's not the woman who was here earlier."

Owens said, "You sure?"

"Positive. Briana was thin and had long red hair. It's not the same woman. I've never seen this woman before."

I dared to scan her body again. Her arms

were flung out as if she'd been trying to catch herself as she fell. Her hands were tanned, with square palms and sturdy fingers.

I said, "Briana had very white skin. Like it never was in the sun."

Owens ran his own plate-sized hand over his face. "Damn."

We all stood for a moment out of an unspoken need to put a space in the time between acknowledging death and attending to it. I moved first.

"Is it okay if I go through the house to get the cats?"

The sergeant's skinny chest rose, taking in air before he moved on to the grisly business at hand. "Don't touch anything. If you see anything you haven't seen before, let me know."

He didn't need to tell me that. It was just something to say to reestablish his authority. I nodded and headed down the hall to look for Elvis and Lucy. My head was buzzing with questions. I knew the assumption would be that Briana had killed the woman, but it takes brute strength to cut another person's throat. Strength and stature. You have to be tall enough to stand behind a person and pull a knife across their throat with enough force to slice their jugular.

Briana had been taller than me, but not much, and she had seemed too soft-boned to make the hard slashing motion it would take to cut deeply into another person's throat. But if Briana hadn't killed the woman on the living room floor, who had? And whether she had or not, where was Briana now?

The Trillins' media room is a movie lover's dream come true — a six-foot screen, plush theater seats, a sound system probably better than the local movie theaters'. The room is also a cat's dream come true. Cupcake and Jancey had designed an intricate overhead system of enclosed tunnels near the ceiling, with lower wide tracks for racing. The tracks led to a tall climbing tree with several branches where the cats could sit and dream or watch movies with their humans. The tree had sisal posts for scratching, padded platforms for sleeping, cubbyholes for hiding, and hanging toys for batting with paws.

I stood under the tree, assembled the folding cat carriers, and sprinkled bonita flake treats in the bottoms.

"Elvis, Lucy, are you up there?"

A soft nicking sound answered, and Lucy's white nose poked through the round hole of one of the condos. Lucy was naturally friendly, but I knew she was more interested in the scent of bonita flakes than in me.

I said, "Hi, sweetheart! Come on down."

After a few more nicking sounds, she oozed out and cantilevered down the tree into my arms. We nuzzled each other until she was purring, and then I lowered her into a carrier and closed it. She made a whirring sound of minor outrage, but Lucy wasn't one to carp about things she couldn't control. I wish I were more like Lucy.

Getting Elvis down took more persuasion. When he finally peered out of the fat tube he was stretched in, I had to stifle a giggle because he had the edge of a crumpled slip of paper in his mouth. Elvis had a fetish about narrow strips of paper that he could easily hold in his mouth. If Cupcake or Jancey tossed a Post-it note or a sales receipt in a wastebasket, Elvis would nab it. If we saw Elvis sitting low with his paws tucked under his chest, we knew he was hiding a slip of paper. He didn't chew it, he just hoarded it, crumpled it, and carried it around in his mouth. I always suspected that he had a stash of papers somewhere that would never be found.

Lucy gave some plaintive bleats that brought Elvis all the way out of his tube.

I said, "Come on down, sweetie."

He blinked at me, sniffed at the scent of bonita flakes, and came down carefully, clutching the tree with all four legs like a possum lowering itself, with a long strip of paper gripped in his teeth. When he was arm high, I lifted him into my arms and told him how wonderful he was, then put him into the other carrier and closed it. I felt like a meanie for tricking the cats, but that's life. Sooner or later, we all get lured by enticing treats and then find ourselves stuck in situations we can't get out of.

At least Elvis still had his precious paper.

3

I made it to the living room just as a team of criminalists outfitted in paper booties and protective smocks came in the front door. They stopped and looked at me with question marks on their faces while I stood there with a cat carrier hanging from each hand like a statue of Cat Lady Justice.

Owens said, "This is Dixie Hemingway. She's a pet sitter. She's going to get the cats out of the way while we work."

As if that cleared *that* up, they all nodded and pulled on latex gloves in preparation for measuring and photographing and probing and all the other things that criminalists do. They would take the temperature of the dead woman's liver to establish how long she'd been dead. They would look for stray hairs or fibers on her skin, her clothing, and the floor. They would scan for footprints and fingerprints, trace the arc of blood spatters and blood flow. They would draw an outline of her body on the floor and photograph it from every angle before they bagged her hands, zipped her into a body bag, and took her to the morgue for a more thorough examination.

Acutely conscious of my unbootied Keds and my unlatexed hands, I mutely circled around them. The cats had gone silent, too. With their keen olfactory sense, they could smell blood through the cardboard of their carriers and had gone into defensive positions with their ears laid back and their backs arched.

At the door, Sergeant Owens caught up with me and spoke in a lowered voice. I didn't know if he spoke quietly out of respect for the dead or because he didn't want the others to hear what he said.

"Dixie, I don't know which detective is going to be handling this, but he'll want to talk to you. Where will you be after you get rid of the cats?"

"I'm not getting *rid* of them, I'm taking them to the Kitty Haven. That's a boardinghouse for cats. After that I'll be at other cats' houses up and down the Key. You have my cell phone number. Call me when you need me."

He considered that and nodded. Maybe I imagined it, but the look he gave me seemed to find my availability downright sad.

I maneuvered myself and the cat carriers through the foyer and out the front door. Deputies had strung yellow police tape around the perimeter of the house and placed a Contamination Sheet on the front door. Every person who entered or exited the house had to sign the sheet and enter the time, so I put the boxes down and signed. It seemed very important at the moment to make it clear that I might be just a pet sitter, but I knew how to conduct myself at a murder scene.

The moment lost some of its drama when I remembered the green-and-whites parked behind my Bronco in the driveway. By the time I'd sweet-talked deputies into moving them so I could leave the scene, I had pulled myself together and stopped feeling like people who solved crimes were more important than people who cleaned litter boxes.

On the way to the Kitty Haven, Elvis and Lucy found their voices and sang to me. Lucy was a coloratura soprano, Elvis was a countertenor. By the time we arrived at the Kitty Haven, I felt as if I'd listened to an entire kitty opera in which two captive royals told the world how maligned they were. Thinking about what was ahead for me and for Cupcake and Jancey made me want to join my own voice to their caterwauling.

I wished Guidry were the detective who was going to be investigating the murder, and not just because I missed him. A new homicide detective who didn't know me would simply look at the fact that I'd been the last person to go into Cupcake's house before the dead woman was found, so I would definitely be given some thought as a suspect. A homicide investigator who'd slept with me would have questioned me, but he'd be less likely to believe I'd had anything to do with the murder.

The thought of the media frenzy the murder would cause made me cringe. When I thought of how newspaper and television reporters would dredge up all the other times I'd been in the news, I felt like throwing up.

It would be even worse for Cupcake and Jancey. The time between reports that a woman had been murdered in their house while they were in Italy and the moment when somebody questioned if Cupcake or Jancey had hired the killer would be about three nanoseconds. The same media that fawns over a famous athlete or movie star will turn on him like rabid wolves if there's a crime involving one of his friends or somebody in his family. Sweet adoration does a U-turn and becomes sour contempt, and all the voices once raised to cheer a star will shriek for that same star's execution. It almost seems as if hidden blood lust is the fuel that creates the cult-worship of the famous. Life might very quickly become a nightmare for Cupcake and Jancey.

And for me.

Siesta Key is eight miles long, north to south. Midnight Pass Road runs end to end, with residential streets looping and winding away from it. Our so-called business district is near the north end of the key where the island bulges to allow greater density. We call that area "the village," as if the restaurants, salons, boutiques, tourist gift shops, and real estate offices aren't a part of the rest of the Key. Siesta Beach stretches along the southern perimeter of the village on Beach Road, and when you drive along there you have to watch for tourists wearing bikinis, straw hats, and bemused smiles crossing against traffic to get to the beach. I think the seaside ions get to them and make them a little loopy.

The Kitty Haven is on Avenida del Mare, about a block off Beach Road, in an old Florida-style frame house. With its sun yellow paint, shiny white hurricane shutters, and white wicker chairs on the deep front porch, it always makes me nostalgic for a time when people sat on porches and chatted over a glass of lemonade.

I parked in the driveway outlined by green and white liriope and lifted the cat carriers out. The cats were poking their noses against the holes in the carriers to sniff the air. I sniffed it a little bit, too. The Kitty Haven's yard is filled with cedar chips interspersed with circles of palm clusters and palmettos, so it smells like the inside of a cedar chest. I carried both cat carriers to the front porch, opened the front door, quickly set one carrier inside, then maneuvered myself and the other carrier in while keeping a sharp eye out for a cat who might decide to streak out while the door was open.

All the guest cats at Kitty Haven have private apartments in the back, but the owner's cats loll on windowsills and drape themselves on overstuffed chairs in the front room. All the furniture is wine red velvet, which always makes me feel as if I've stepped into a bordello in an Old West movie. The cat hair on the velvet gives it a kind of halo effect.

A bell over the door announced my arrival, and Marge Preston bustled from the back surrounded by the same halo. Like her velvet chairs, Marge is plump and soft, and her fine white hair stands out around her face like cat whiskers.

I said, "Marge, I have a bit of an emergency here. There was an incident in their house and the police are there, so I had to get them out fast."

As if she was accustomed to people bringing cats to her because "an incident" had happened in their home, Marge didn't bat an eye.

I said, "Their owners are in Italy, but they're going to come home as soon as they can. Their names are Elvis and Lucy."

"The owners?"

"No, the cats. You can use my name as the owner."

That got a raised eyebrow. "So their owner is somebody famous?"

I grinned. "Somebody anonymous."

Marge knelt to open Lucy's case, and Lucy raised her head to sniff at Marge's fingertips.

I said, "Lucy makes friends a little faster than Elvis, but they're both very sweet cats."

Marge lifted both cats out and cradled one in each arm. They both went limp with trust. Marge brings that out in a cat.

She said, "Any special needs?"

"No, they're easy. I'll let you know when

the owners will be back."

I was already backing toward the front door, ready to hightail it to my other clients.

Marge said, "Take the carriers with you."

Chastened, I came back to collect the carriers. I didn't take time to fold them, just carried them out and tossed them in the back of the Bronco to use when I brought the cats home. Elvis had left his scrap of paper in his carrier, and I grinned to myself when I thought how put out he would be when he remembered it.

The delay at Cupcake's house had thrown me an hour late. On an ordinary day, I get up at 4:00 A.M. and see eight or nine pets, spending about thirty minutes at each house. With travel time and the occasional delay, my morning visits are usually over by nine or nine thirty, and by then I'm starved for breakfast and sleep. Now it was already close to eight o'clock, and I still had four pet visits to make, some with multiple pets in one house. On top of that, I would have to give an interview to a new homicide detective. It was going to be a long morning.

I didn't realize I was being tailed until I left the second house of the four on my list. I had turned onto Midnight Pass Road, and a white Jaguar convertible I'd seen behind me earlier swung too close behind me. Convertibles aren't good choices for tailing somebody. The woman driver was clearly visible. Her head was snugly wrapped in a printed scarf, and she wore huge dark shades, but she was definitely a woman. A pale woman with bright red lipstick. I couldn't see her fingernails, but I would have bet good money that the hands with a death grip on the steering wheel had scarlet fingertips.

I said, "Oh, great! That's just *terrific!*"

My first thought was that Briana had switched from stalking Cupcake to stalking me, which had a kind of sick glamour to it. My second thought was that Briana had just killed a woman in Cupcake's house, which detracted a lot from the sick glamour.

Instinctively, my hand went to my cell phone to call Guidry and tell him the woman who'd murdered another woman in Cupcake Trillin's house was following me. But then I remembered that Guidry had gone away. The murder wasn't his problem, and neither was I.

The car in front of me stopped for a red light, and I oozed to a stop behind its bumper. The Jaguar jerked to a stop, and the driver threw open the door and ran toward the passenger door of the Bronco. I could have locked the door. To this day, I don't know why I sat there like a dope and let Briana hurl herself into the seat beside me. She wore a thin white linen shirt hanging loose over slubby white linen pants, but she wasn't naked under them. In fact, the lace bra under her shirt seemed designed to be seen. The bra probably had an Italian label and cost as much as my Bronco.

She seemed more afraid of me than I was of her.

"Please," she said. "I need help. As Cupcake's friend, I'm begging you."

I said, "In the first place, you're not Cupcake's friend. You're a stalker who broke into his house and killed somebody. In the second place, I'm a pet sitter, not somebody who can give you help."

Her red lips pushed out in the way lips do when people are confused. "I meant *you* were Cupcake's friend."

"Well, that's true. But I can't help you."

"You're the only one who *can* help me! And I didn't kill anybody! I know it looks that way, but I swear I didn't do it!"

I am both blessed and cursed with an uncanny ability to tell when a person is lying. I don't know if it's some genetic trait or the fact that I had an alcoholic mother who lied as skillfully as she put on lipstick.

Whatever the reason, I'm sort of a flesh-and-blood lie detector machine, and I didn't think Briana was lying. I thought she was a complete kook, a neurotic bundle of fantasies, an immature woman crammed with silly dreams, but I didn't believe she was a killer.

The light turned green, and cars behind me began to honk. Briana opened the Bronco's door and got out, but turned back with a pleading look that would have melted a steel beam. My mind whirled with ideas, each of which I rejected before it was completed.

I said, "Look, I have to take care of some pets. I'll be finished in about an hour and a half. Meet me at the pavilion at Siesta Beach."

She half-sobbed, "Thank you!" and slammed the door shut.

As I drove on, I watched in the rearview mirror as she sprinted to the Jaguar. My hands were calm on the steering wheel, but my brain was in utter chaos. It screamed that I was the dumbest, weirdest, craziest person in the universe. It hollered that I should call Sergeant Owens and tell him where Briana was. It thundered that talking to Briana was a form of betrayal. A betrayal of the faith Sergeant Owens had in me, of the faith Cupcake and Jancey had in me, of the faith *I* had in me. Everything it said was true.

I told myself I should have nothing to do with the situation. The homicide detective handling the case might not have Guidry's sharp intelligence, but my sole responsibility was to see that Elvis and Lucy were cared for. I should pick up the phone and call Sergeant Owens and not even think about keeping my promise to Briana to talk to her.

But the entire time I was telling myself all that, I was remembering a time in my own life when I had teetered on the edge of insanity. I had never been so crazy that I'd become delusional like Briana, but perhaps whatever had happened in Cupcake's house had snapped her back to normal and she was scrambling to claw her way back to the real world. When I had been crazy, kind people had offered me the hand I needed to get back to myself. Briana had reached out to me, and it seemed to me that it would be hypocritical to turn her down since I had once been in such need of help myself.

While I had that internal debate with myself, I continued driving without calling Sergeant Owens. As if I was being moved by forces outside myself. As if it wasn't my choice to cross a line from which there would be no return.

Funny how we can play games with ourselves like that.

4

On ordinary days, I have breakfast at the Village Diner after I've finished my morning rounds. But this wasn't an ordinary day. This was a day when I'd stupidly made an appointment with a famous model who was a prime murder suspect. Nevertheless, I was famished, so I crossed the north bridge to the mainland and hurried into Morton's Gourmet Market, where the sandwich guy is nice enough to custom-make my favorite sandwich in all the world: baked turkey breast on pumpernickel bread with fresh tarragon mayonnaise.

While he stacked layers of turkey on dark bread, I filled a large to-go cup with coffee and went to the bakery department and asked for a fruit tartlet. As the bakery woman handed over the tartlet in its little see-through box, she said, "Anything else?"

I shook my head, then wondered if Briana had eaten breakfast. It's a curse I have. Like my brother, I want to make sure nobody in the world goes hungry. Unlike him, I don't want to cook for people, I just want to see them eat.

I said, "Um, make that two tartlets."

I filled another big cup with coffee and went back to the sandwich counter, where my turkey on pumpernickel waited.

I said, "I need another one, please. And two large pickles."

The sandwich guy turned to build another one, and I snagged two bags of chips from a rack. I was now doubly wrong. I was not only guilty of planning a secret meeting with a woman wanted for murder, I intended to feed her.

A sweet-faced woman stepped to the deli counter between two little girls, each gripping one of her hands as if she were a maypole. Identical twins, the girls looked to be about six years old, the age Christy would have been if she'd lived. I had a momentary hardening of veins and muscles and lungs, an involuntary blend of rage and yearning and jealousy that this woman had two children and I had none.

The sandwich man said, "Looks like you need something to carry all that in."

While I forced myself back to sensibility, he went to some other part of the store and came back with a neat cardboard tray big enough for sandwich cartons, tartlet cartons, and chips, with cutouts for the two coffees.

I thanked him profusely, smiled at the cute little girls, and carried the tray to the Bronco filled with admiration for the unsung people who recognize homely needs and fill them with clever inventions like carry-out trays.

It's only a quick scoot from Morton's across the bridge and around to Siesta Beach. As I carried the clever cardboard tray and its goodies up the steps to the pavilion area, I realized that I didn't really expect Briana to meet me there. She might be crazy, but she would expect me to be smart enough to alert the sheriff's department about our meeting. Even if she had figured out that I was dumb enough not to call them, she would have realized by now that she had mistaken Cupcake's cat sitter for a person with his importance and power. She would know I couldn't do a thing for her.

Realizing that was a big relief. I could relax under the shade of the pavilion roof and have breakfast in solitude. I would eat one of the turkey sandwiches and drink one of the coffees, and if I wanted more coffee I could drink Briana's. I would eat my tartlet and save the other for later. And when I left, I would offer Briana's sandwich and chips to some young person who looked hungry and broke. I was not only going to enjoy a meal at the beach, I would have the pleasure of giving away food. I was Lady Bountiful in cat-hairy shorts.

A woman at one of the tables waved to me. I stopped with the little cardboard tray clutched close to my chest and peered at her. She had removed the scarf from around her head and stuffed all her red hair up under a big floppy white hat. She still wore the huge dark shades, and her lips were still bright red. She stood up and walked toward me. She moved with that sharp-shouldered, flat-assed, pointy-toed, pelvic-bone thrust that runway models use. Anybody watching her walk would know her purpose in life was to make very expensive clothes look tantalizingly desirable to very rich women.

I never felt so dowdy and fleshy in my life.

I frowned sternly at her. "Sit down! Don't attract attention."

"Oh, I'm sorry!"

She stylishly scurried back to her table while I clumped after her with my stupid cardboard tray pressed against my low-class bosom.

She didn't even look around for law

enforcement officers when I sat down across from her. She was either the most naive woman in the world or so arrogantly sure of herself that she assumed I wouldn't have given her away.

I said, "I brought you a sandwich and coffee."

Her red lips pursed as if she had to think about what to say. "I suppose I should eat."

I nodded vigorously and handed over her sandwich.

"Look, I don't know what you hope to accomplish by talking to me, but you have to know you're going to be arrested."

Her hand was fish-belly white, with long boneless fingers. Her red nails picked at the wrapper on the sandwich and peeled it away as delicately as a cat separating what it will eat from what it disdains.

She said, "I don't think Cupcake will have me arrested. He's too sweet to want me in jail."

I whipped the wrapper off my own sandwich and took a big bite. I chewed slowly, looking at her as if she were a skinny white shark that had just washed up on the beach.

I swallowed. I took a swig of coffee. She was still uncovering the mystery of her sandwich.

I said, "It's not so much what Cupcake

wants done about you. There's the little matter of a murdered woman. The law gets pretty worked up about murder. They'll want to know what happened in Cupcake's house, how that woman's throat got cut."

Briana finished folding the wrapper back from her sandwich. She raised it to her red lips and took little rabbit nibbles at it. Her teeth were so chalk white, I almost expected them to crumble to powder from the pressure.

She said, "I'll just explain to them that I don't know. After you left, I knew people would come to make me leave the house, so I went to the master bedroom and changed clothes. When I came out, a bleeding woman was lying on the living room floor. I was afraid, and I ran out the back door."

Jancey was going to be really steamed that Briana had used their bedroom.

I said, "That's your story?"

"It's the truth."

"Briana, nobody in the world will believe that."

"They will if you help me convince them."

I chewed some more and told myself to keep my voice down, not to yell at her, not to stand up and shout, "Are you completely nuts?" because in fact she was completely nuts, and it wouldn't change anything to point it out to her.

I said, "Let's start at the beginning. How did you get into the Trillins' house?"

She waved a languid hand. "Oh, that was easy. I have a little handheld electronic gizmo that can disengage selected zones of the security system without alerting the security company. I blocked the zone that regulates the scanners outside the back sliding patio door. All I had to do was pick the lock. Took about ten seconds."

Her voice had gone brisk and sure of itself. I didn't know if what she described was possible, but she sure sounded like she knew what she was talking about.

"What about the entrance gate? What about the walls around the whole place?"

She smiled. "Parked my Jag out of sight on the other side of the wall, climbed up and clipped the razor ribbon hidden under the vines, pushed it aside, tossed a plastic ladder over, and came over. I hid the ladder behind the vines so I could climb back up. The wall where I cut the wire is behind some trees, and nobody pays any attention to a woman jogging early in the morning."

My hand holding my sandwich sank to the table. This woman was not a dithery nut. She was an accomplished break-in artist, a calculating scaler of razor-topped walls, a woman with wire clippers and experience at slipping into places impassible to everybody else.

"I take it this isn't your first breaking-and-entering job."

That smile again, cool and sure of itself. "Hardly."

"You supplement your modeling income with a little theft on the side?"

This time she actually chuckled, as if she found me drolly amusing. "I go in people's houses, but I don't steal anything. I just like to get a look at other people's private lives. You might say it's a hobby, like stamp collecting or softball."

"Okay, so you didn't break into Cupcake's house to steal. What was your reason? Why were you stalking him?"

Her smug smile died. "Is that what he thinks? That I was *stalking* him?"

I couldn't keep my mouth from saying it anymore. "Are you *nuts?* Of course that's what he thinks!"

Her red mouth turned down at the corners. It trembled. She raised her fingers to her lips to comfort them. A tear trickled down her cheek from behind the dark shades. Her shoulders sagged as if a great weight had been laid on them.

"I thought he would understand. Of all

the people in the world, I trusted Cupcake to understand."

My own shoulders went a few inches lower, too. Whatever the woman carried around in her disturbed head sent out heavy, oppressive waves.

I said, "Here's the deal, Briana. A woman was murdered inside the home of Cupcake and Jancey Trillin. You were in the house at the time the woman was killed. Now you say you have a history of breaking and entering. If you think I'm going to be moved by some sentimental crap about your mystical connection with Cupcake, you underestimate my intelligence. Unless you have a credible explanation for what happened — other than 'she was already dead when I walked in on her' — I'm out of here and you're on your own."

Her head raised, and I could feel anger in the eyes behind the sunshades. But she must have heard reality in what I'd said, because she sighed and pushed her sandwich aside as if she were clearing the deck to get down to business.

"I've known Cupcake Trillin practically all my life. We lived in a little parish in Louisiana where half the population is below the poverty line. Women marry in their teens, have a passel of babies by the time they're twenty, fry up fish their men catch in the bayous, grow old fast from worry and work. Men, especially black men, work in sugar-cane fields the same way Appalachian men work in coal mines. It's what their fathers and grandfathers have always done, and unless they're extra smart or extra talented, it's what they'll do, too."

Her voice trembled, and she took a sip of coffee.

"I make it sound as if it was all grim, but I have good memories, too. Like the man who came to our back door twice a week selling fresh fish from an ice-filled box on the back of his truck. He sold shrimp, too, right off the boats. At certain times of the year, he had crawfish, and my folks would order fifty pounds and have a party. They boiled the crawfish in huge pots with lots of cayenne pepper thrown in to make the crayfish spit out the sand. All their friends would gather in the backyard, and we'd suck meat from crawfish tails and drink cold beer."

I made a get-on-with-it motion, and her pale skin flushed pink.

"Cupcake and I were the odd ones in our families. We didn't fit in, didn't want the same things they wanted for us. It was the same way in school. We were smarter than most everybody else, including the teachers. And we laughed at things the other kids thought were holy and important. Nobody else wanted us, so we sort of drifted together."

"You were friends?"

"More than friends."

"Lovers?"

That faint blush again. "We weren't like that. We just sort of dared each other to go beyond what the world expected and then supported each other while we did it."

She let a beat go by as if she were watching images float by inside her head.

She said, "I would have followed the devil himself if he'd offered me a chance to get out of that little town." She stopped and flashed an ironic smile. "Perhaps I did."

I looked at the eyeball-sized emerald on her hand and thought that the devil was certainly generous.

She said, "Cupcake escaped because he was an outstanding athlete. I escaped by leaving my family and everything I knew, and I've never been back."

"You just left? Just like that?"

Her lips tightened. "Sorry. The truth doesn't come easily. I've lied so much about my family I've almost come to believe my own lies. My official bio says I was orphaned in a little village in Switzerland when my parents were killed in an avalanche, but a kind couple adopted me and brought me to the United States. Minnesota, to be exact. I say I grew up on a remote farm and that my adoptive parents home-schooled me until I was eighteen and then I left home with their blessings. The truth is I was born in Louisiana on the fork of the Mississippi River to a couple who never went beyond grade school and had about six teeth between them. My white-trash uncle molested me from the time I was six. I killed him when I was sixteen. Shot him through the head with a double-barreled shotgun my father used for killing rattlesnakes. Then I took off. Worked as a maid for a while, turned some tricks, and then got discovered by a modeling agency."

Her voice had the gritty underpinning of harsh truth.

I said, "You left out the part about breaking into people's houses."

She took a deep breath. "That's how Cupcake and I got the money for books and shoes, clothes, haircuts, things we couldn't have had otherwise." With a sly smile, she said, "Cupcake mostly did it so he could buy a pair of Nikes."

My jaw dropped. Cupcake was the most

honest man I knew.

She grinned. "We were very young then. And we never took anything truly valuable. We wouldn't have recognized anything valuable anyway, and the fence we took things to insisted that we stick to small things that he could sell easily."

"That's how you learned to break through security systems?"

"No, that came later. Cupcake didn't have anything to do with that. I learned all that on my own."

I could feel my cheeks firm up, the way a face does when it's trying not to show shock or disgust.

She said, "After I left the parish, I never had any contact with Cupcake, but I followed his career. He was the only person in my life I could depend on to always be kind to me."

"So you showed your appreciation by coming here and breaking into his house?"

Her lips trembled. "You can't know what it's like to be famous. To be *Briana.* Everybody in the world wants something from me. I haven't lived my own life for a long time. I've lived for agents, accountants, photographers, designers, reporters, all those people sucking my breath out of my body. I started remembering what it was like when it was just me and Cupcake against the world. I didn't really think I could make that happen, but I wanted to be close to him, just absorb some of his kindness and calm. I knew he was away from home at the camp he runs for kids. I didn't think it would hurt anybody if I borrowed his life for a while. Until you walked in, I was like a kid playing house. I guess I took it too far."

She was right in thinking that Cupcake's plans had been to spend time at the kids' camp. That had been reported in the news, and I didn't correct her about where he'd really been.

I had a feeling that Briana had left out a lot of her history, but I believed parts of what she'd told me. Fame is hard for anybody to handle, even mature people with firm philosophies. For a poor, uneducated, sexually molested small-town girl who'd had to use every wile and wit she had to escape a life of grinding poverty, it would have been a crushing assault.

Nevertheless, she had not explained the dead woman in Cupcake's house — and the more I listened to her, the farther I crawled into a dark tunnel that had no exit.

5

I said, "Okay, I'll buy the reason you were in Cupcake's house. Now tell me about the woman."

She leaned closer to me. "I swear to you I don't know who she was. I'm telling the truth about finding her dead on the floor when I came back from the bedroom."

"And you just bolted and ran?"

She hesitated. "I took time to restore the security system after I was away from the back door." Her voice had risen an octave.

With great deliberation, I took my tartlet from its little clear box and took a bite. I studied her face while I chewed. Her face went pink while I washed the tartlet bite down with coffee.

I said, "You're lying."

"I swear it's the truth."

"Considering your track record when it comes to truth, I'm not moved."

I couldn't see her eyes, but I knew they

were fixed on me, waiting for me to dissect her lie. Only problem was, I didn't know what her lie had been. Growing up with an alcoholic mother whose lies had slid all over the place, I'd learned early to detect the presence of an untruth in the midst of candor, but it was like a whiff of something gone bad in a refrigerator full of good food. You know something in there is spoiled, but you don't know what it is. I still believed somebody else had killed the woman in Cupcake's house, but either Briana had lied about not recognizing the woman or she had lied about when and how she'd run away from the house.

I said, "If you didn't kill the woman, then somebody else was in the house while you were there."

She shook her head too emphatically. "I was alone."

"You think the woman slit her own throat? Disposed of the knife before she fell dead? Damned clever of her."

She took a deep breath and exhaled in jerky bursts of air. "I meant I didn't have a companion. Somebody else must have broken in while I was there, and I didn't know about it."

"If that had happened, the security company would have got an alarm and sent somebody to investigate. Nobody came."

"I'm telling the truth."

I finished my fruit tartlet and considered what to do next. I had to call Sergeant Owens. I had to call Cupcake and Jancey. I had to tell them that I'd talked to Briana without anybody's permission. I fervently wished I'd never done it. In probing Briana's story, I'd found out things about Cupcake that he probably didn't want known. Even worse, I'd provided a dress rehearsal for the interrogation she'd get from the sheriff's department. My questions had given Briana a heads-up on what the homicide detective — whoever that was going to be — would ask her. Because I had felt empathy for a woman I'd thought was deranged, I might have skewed a murder investigation.

She said, "Are you going to betray me?"

The question was so stark and direct that it took me by surprise. That may be one of the differences between people who have the drive and determination to be internationally famous and the rest of us. Along with the drive comes a loss of social subterfuge.

I said, "I'm not the only person who's seen you. It's inevitable that somebody will recognize you. But they won't call the cops, they'll call *USA Today* or Katie Couric. And when they do, you'll be stuck knowing that somebody used you for their own gain, and it'll make you even less willing to trust people."

"Psychology so early in the morning. And from a pet sitter, no less."

"Most people believe fashion models have the brains of a flea. Those same people belittle the intelligence of pet sitters."

She colored. "I'm sorry. And you're right. Every time I'm hurt I grow more paranoid."

I said, "Do you have a lawyer?"

"Just one who handles contracts."

"Do you know a defense lawyer?"

She shook her head, and even her hands turned paler. "Do you know one?"

I thought of Ethan Crane, and just the thought of him made me feel lighter. Suddenly moving with quick efficiency, I whipped out my cell phone and dialed Ethan's number.

When his receptionist answered, I said, "Tell Mr. Crane that Dixie Hemingway has an emergency and will be at his office in five minutes."

Doubtfully, she said, "I'll tell him, but I'm not sure —"

All I'd wanted to know was whether Ethan was in, so I clicked her off and crammed our cups and sandwich leavings — Briana had barely touched her sandwich, and she didn't even open her tartlet box — into the cardboard tray. Briana watched me get up and toss the tray into a trash bin, watched me walk back to our table.

I said, "I'm going to drive to the office of an attorney I know. If you choose to, you can follow me and go in with me and tell your story. If you choose not to, we're done."

I spun around and did a fast clip out of the pavilion and down the steps to the parking lot. I got in my Bronco while Briana made a white blur behind me charging to her Jaguar. The woman could move fast when she wanted to. I peeled out, and the Jag kept up. I was both glad and disappointed that she was sticking to me. It would go a lot better for her if she got a lawyer and turned herself in. It would go a lot better for me if she ditched me and ran.

I should be ashamed to admit it, but the reason my blood tingled on the way to Ethan Crane's office wasn't solely from guilty excitement at being on the sidelines of a murder investigation. My blood always tingled like that when I thought of Ethan. I hadn't seen him for a good while, and then just briefly in the parking lot of the Village Diner, but Ethan and I had always set off lust sparks in each other. There had been a time when I'd had to make a decision about pursuing romantic possibilities with Ethan, but I had wanted Guidry's slightly dangerous company more than Ethan's reliable solidness.

Ethan's office occupies one of the old sand-softened stucco buildings in the village. He inherited the building and the law practice from his grandfather and has never seen fit to modernize any of it. The entrance door from the sidewalk has a glass top with flaked gilt lettering reading ETHAN CRANE, ESQ. A cramped foyer is mostly taken up by a wide staircase leading to the second floor. The dark wooden steps are thinner and paler at their centers from generations of feet stepping on them. At the top of the stairs, a wide lobby separates a receptionist's office from a library and conference room. Ethan's office is at the back of the lobby. If his door is open, he can see anybody who climbs the stairs.

His door was open. An old oaken hat rack with a rung for umbrellas stands in the corner of his office. When Ethan works at his desk, he removes his suit jacket and hangs it neatly on a wooden hanger from the rack. But as reassuring evidence that his receptionist had given him warning that I was coming and that he welcomed my visit, his dark pinstripe jacket sat nattily on his broad shoulders, his silk rep tie was neatly in place, and the edges of his white shirt cuffs made thin rims at the end of his sleeves. I was sure he wore tasteful cufflinks.

He stood when he saw me, then lifted a dark eyebrow when Briana chugged up the stairs behind me.

By any standard, Ethan is one of the handsomest men on the planet. A fraction of Seminole blood gives him bronze skin, dark, deep-set eyes, straight black hair cut to brush his shirt collar, a proud nose, prominent cheekbones, and lips made for kissing. His smile is white and even, his voice sounds like the velvet male speaker on credit card commercials, and I can attest from personal experience that his kisses make you lose any sense you ever had.

From her side office, the receptionist bleated some words I ignored. I was too intent on the pleasure on Ethan's face at seeing me. All the old emotions whirled and tugged at me, including my sense of unfamiliarity with all the tradition and history in the shelves of law books and the old butt-worn wooden chairs in front of the grandfather's huge mahogany desk. Ethan moved out from behind his desk and met me halfway in his office.

Not for the first time, I noticed that he had beautiful ears, and that they were gently cupped to hear every word that fell from my lips. I had an almost irresistible urge to rise up on tiptoe and run my tongue around the rim of one. Not to start anything, just to lick it the way babies lick things that appeal to them. It's downright disgusting what some of my body parts do in their imagination.

My face must have shown something of how I felt, because one corner of his very fine lips lifted and little smile lines appeared at the side as if they were etched there by habit. Dang, I had to get my mind on why I was there.

He took both my hands in his. "Dixie. It's good to see you."

To my utter surprise, I felt tears sting my eyelids, and for a second I couldn't get my tongue to work.

He said, "I hear you have an emergency. What can I do for you?"

Oh, yeah. I was there for Briana, not to rekindle an old lust.

I nodded toward Briana, who had removed her big hat so her red hair tumbled over her shoulders. She had removed her dark glasses, too. Her eyes were tawny, like a lion's.

"The emergency is actually hers. She's a prime suspect in a murder. I know it will be better if she has an attorney when she turns herself in."

"I'm not a criminal lawyer."

As if she'd heard a musical cue, Briana stepped forward with her hand out, elegant and assured as all hell. "Thank you so much for seeing me, Ethan. I'm Briana."

Ethan quirked an eyebrow again.

I said, "Briana only uses the one name, like Cher. She's a famous model."

In Briana's aura, I felt dumpy and used up, like the mother of a homecoming queen.

Ethan took a deep breath, and I knew he was feeling that I only thought of him as someone to solve a problem or provide sensible direction. That wasn't true. I thought of him in plenty of other ways that I didn't want him to guess, but I understood why he'd think that.

He gestured toward the chairs facing his desk. "Tell me the situation."

Briana and I took seats, but it was Briana's situation, and I waited for her to talk.

She said, "This is difficult."

Neither Ethan nor I said anything to make it easier, so she straightened her back and tilted herself slightly forward toward Ethan as if to make her words more intimate.

"The truth is that I went into a house without the owner's permission. I knew he and his wife were away, and I went in and walked around inside his house. I should not have done that, but I did not steal anything, and I had no motive except to be in the home of a man I'd known when I was very young. While I was there, Dixie came into the house."

She turned and looked at me with those yellow-brown eyes. "I suppose Dixie has a key." The inflection said she wasn't at all sure I had a key, and that perhaps I'd broken in the same way she had.

I spoke to Ethan. "I'm taking care of the cats in the house. The house, by the way, belongs to Cupcake Trillin. He's an —"

Ethan completed my sentence, as if everybody in the world, not just sports fans, knew who Cupcake was. "Inside linebacker for the Bucs."

He digested that bit of information and nodded for Briana to continue.

"Dixie left, and I knew she would call the police, so I ran to the bedroom and got dressed." She allowed herself a faint smile. "I was more or less nude when Dixie came in." The invitation to Ethan was almost spoken: *Imagine me naked!*

Ethan's face didn't change. His dark eyes were flat. Briana looked down at her twisted hands as if she were unaccustomed to getting no response from a man.

In a rush, she said, "When I went back to the living room, a woman was on the floor. Her throat had been cut and blood was gushing out. Blood was all over her, all over the floor, it was terrible. I was terrified. I ran. I didn't see anybody else, but somebody else had to be there. I ran out of the house. I ran to my car. I waited out of sight until I saw Dixie's car leave the gate into the neighborhood, then I followed her. I knew I would be a suspect. I didn't know what to do. Reporters will want to talk to me, photographers, everything I've been trying to escape. Dixie stopped at a light, and I got out and ran to her car and begged her to help me. She was an angel. She met me and I told her my story and she believed me."

Ethan's eyes flicked to me, and my face went hot.

"She left out a good bit of the story, but I believed enough of it to advise her to get a lawyer and turn herself in."

He said, "Good advice."

Briana said, "Can you keep this out of the

press? It will be hell if it hits the news!"

Ethan raised that eyebrow. "A murder in the home of a famous athlete?"

She said, "I meant about me."

Ethan leaned toward her, but not in the intimate way she'd tilted herself toward him. His was more like a ship's prow aiming at a curl of froth thrown up by a sea wave.

"I'm afraid you lost any right to anonymity the moment you broke into the Trillins' house. You might as well get prepared to give some straight answers to solid questions. And you can begin by providing your last name."

"I didn't kill that woman! I swear to God I didn't kill that woman!"

"And your last name is?"

Briana's lips squeezed together so tightly that her cheeks took on the creases she might have in half a century. Ethan studied her the way he would study a law book.

He said, "Here's the way the district attorney is going to see this case: You're a celebrity whose fame comes solely from modeling designer clothes. You don't have any other talents, but you think your fame gives you special privileges. You broke into a house while the owners were away. Someone authorized to be there came in the house, found you, and pulled out her phone to call the police. You hit her over the head and knocked her out. You knew she would wake up and the world would know what you'd done, so you slit her throat. Then you ran."

He leaned back in his chair. "Refusing to give your last name is not only a silly bit of celebrity branding, it means you're so certain of your privileged status that you expect to smile prettily, flirt a little bit, and skip back to your glamorous world. But Briana, my dear, it's not going to be that way. You're in for the fight of your life, and if you're planning on playing it cute and coy, you'll lose."

I felt as if a boxcar filled with ice had just been dumped on me. Ethan's description of what might have happened seemed so plausible that I was amazed I hadn't seen it like that myself. I had been so focused on the idea of a killer cutting the woman's throat from behind that I hadn't realized she could have been unconscious and stretched on the floor. Briana was certainly big enough and strong enough to have squatted beside her and slit her throat.

Briana's hands gripped the mahogany arms of her chair so tightly her knuckles gleamed like white bone. With visible effort, she parted her lips and said, "Weiland."

Ethan said, "Spelling?"

She spelled it with a sound of weariness. "W-E-I-L-A-N-D."

Ethan said, "And you're from?"

I felt like raising my hand and saying, "I know! I know!" because I knew she came from the same little swampy Louisiana town that Cupcake was from.

She said, "Switzerland. My parents were killed when I was a child. I was adopted by Americans from Minnesota. They're also dead."

She didn't look at me. She was cool as a Popsicle. She sounded as if she absolutely believed every word she said, the same way she had sounded when she'd told me she was Cupcake's wife. The woman was either so crazy she believed every lie she told, or she was an Oscar-level actor. Or both.

Ethan took a slim leather directory from his desk drawer and flipped through it looking for a number. When he found it, he punched it into his phone. While the call went through, he got up and walked out of the office. We couldn't hear his conversation, but I knew he was calling a defense attorney.

Briana's head was high, and she still hadn't looked at me.

She said, "When you talk to Cupcake, please tell him I'm very, very sorry."

6

I left Ethan's office feeling awful. He had made an afternoon appointment for Briana to see a defense attorney whose name I'd heard in connection with wealthy people who'd been accused of major crimes — the ones you instantly assume are guilty as hell but will walk because they have the money for a smart attorney. I didn't know anymore what I thought of Briana's guilt or innocence. One minute I believed she really had found the murdered woman already dead. The next moment I wasn't so sure.

But that wasn't what made me feel wretched.

The thing that made me feel as if some tarry monster were sucking at my breath was that I had sat quietly and let Briana protect Cupcake by telling her professional lie about being from Switzerland with conveniently dead Swiss parents and adoptive American parents. I hadn't spoken up because I'd wanted to protect Cupcake, too.

Worse than that, the man I liked so much that I'd kept my mouth shut for him was also a liar. He had lied not only to me but to his wife. He had pretended to be completely at a loss to understand why Briana had been stalking him. He'd played the big innocent, when all the time he'd known Briana since he was a boy. He'd even broken into houses and stolen things with her. You can't get much more intimate with another person than to commit a crime together. Even though they'd been kids at the time, that would have forged a guilty connection he wouldn't have forgotten.

Knowing that Cupcake had lied about knowing Briana made me question him in a way I hated. I liked Cupcake more than most anybody I knew. I knew him to be loyal to his friends and levelheaded and fair, even with people who didn't deserve fairness. He had the physique of a granite mountain and a scowly face guaranteed to scare people, but underneath all that hardness was a sentimental streak as sweet as the smile that had earned him the name Cupcake. He was one of my heroes, and I felt sick every time I remembered the colossal lie he'd told about knowing Briana. I felt even sicker at the fact that I would have to confront him with the lie. I hated to think what would happen when Jancey found out.

By the time I got home, I was exhausted not only from being up since 4:00 A.M. but from my own dark thoughts.

Siesta Key's shape is a bit like a cigar with a bulge at the northern end. The Gulf of Mexico is to the west and Sarasota Bay to the east. I live in an apartment on the south end on the Gulf side. My apartment is above a four-slot carport at the end of a twisting shelled driveway lined with mossy oaks, pines, sea grape, and palms. A deck lies behind the carport, and the deck is attached to a frame house my grandparents bought from the Sears, Roebuck catalog. They raised my mother there, but she never loved the Key the way her parents did. She married a firefighter and had my brother and me, but she never loved us either. She left us after our dad died putting out a fire, and Michael and I moved into the house with our grandparents.

So many relatives from the North showed up every summer that my grandfather built the garage apartment as a guesthouse. Now it's my home. I moved in after my husband and little girl were killed in a freak accident. Michael and his partner, Paco, had already moved into the house after our grandparents died, so now we're all here in our own little private gulfside compound, secure in the sound of surf and sea gulls.

Except for Paco's Harley, all the car slots were empty when I got home. Michael was on duty at the firehouse, and God knew where Paco was. Michael is a fireman like our dad was, so he works twenty-four/forty-eight — twenty-four-hour shifts with forty-eight-hour breaks. Paco is with the Sarasota County's Special Investigative Bureau, so his work schedule depends on whatever undercover operation he's in. Michael and I don't ask him about his work. In the first place, he wouldn't tell us. In the second place, it would make us worry if we knew, so we just don't.

I eased my Bronco into its space and got out into steamy noontime heat. The parakeets had retreated into the shadows of treetops for a siesta. A few gulls trudged along the edge of the shoreline making halfhearted pecks at microscopic sea life in the frothy edges of the surf, but they looked as if they were ready for naps, too. All intelligent life in Florida naps in the middle of the day.

As I climbed the stairs to the porch, I used the remote to raise the metal hurricane shutters on my apartment's French doors.

The doors are the only entry to my apartment, so the shutters double as security bars. Since our place sits off the beaten track in secluded privacy, we have to think about things like that. The porch has a deep roof and runs the length of the apartment. Two ceiling fans are there to move the air when I sit outside, and a hammock is strung in one corner in case I want to fall into it. There's also a glass-topped table with two chairs where I can sit and look out at sailboats in the Gulf.

When I got to the top of the stairs, I saw Ella Fitzgerald inside looking through the glass on the door. Ella is a true calico Persian mix, meaning she's part Persian and that her fur has distinct red, black, and white blocks of color. She's named for Ella Fitzgerald because she makes funny scatting sounds. Officially, Ella was a gift to me, but she'd had the same flutter-lash reaction to Michael and Paco that most females have, so she's more theirs than mine now. I groom her and take care of her when they're on duty, but she considers Michael's kitchen her real home. Pretty smart of her, too.

I opened the French doors and picked Ella up and smooched the top of her head.

She said, "Thrrrrrppp!"

I walked through my minuscule living

room into my equally minuscule bedroom and threw my shoulder bag on the bed.

I said, "You're right, I'm late. I had a little problem this morning."

She smiled at me and nosed at my chin. There is just nothing in the world like a cat wanting to kiss your chin to make you feel that the world may turn out okay after all.

I put her on the bed beside my bag and started peeling off my clothes. I pushed my shorts down and said, "You won't believe this, but somebody got murdered in Cupcake Trillin's house, and it happened while I was there."

She did her *thrrpp!* thing.

While I fought my sleeveless T-shirt over my head, I muffled, "A woman was in the house."

Ella turned her head to follow the arc of the shirt as it sailed onto the bed.

I stepped out of my bikini underpants. "Not the woman who was killed, but another woman."

I twisted my bra around to the front and unhooked it. "She's a famous model named Briana. She has always told the press that she's from Switzerland, but she lied."

I shook my bra at Ella. "Cupcake claims he doesn't know her, but she says they went to school together. Do you have any idea what Jancey will do if she finds out Cupcake lied about knowing Briana?"

Ella's eyes rounded in alarm. "Nik!"

"Boy, you got that right! She will be pissed nine ways from Thursday, and she'll have every right to be. I don't know why he lied. It doesn't make any sense."

I kicked off my Keds and gathered up all my clothes and padded naked to the washer and dryer in the hall alcove. I shoved everything in and added detergent.

I muttered, "Briana says she doesn't know who the dead woman was, but I'm not sure if that's the truth." Still muttering, I went into the bathroom and turned on the shower. As soon as water splashed on me, I shut up and enjoyed.

Personally, I think water was one of God's best jobs. He gets five stars for trees, too, and no question that sunshine was way up there as an accomplishment. Animals, too, even reptiles, which I don't personally care for but have nothing against as a race. He sort of slipped a little bit on creating humans, but I suppose in his infinite wisdom he had good reason for making some of them complete asses. But water is so wonderful that if God hadn't created it I'd have tried to do it myself. I can feel like fifteen different kinds of crap and go stand under a warm shower and by the time I get out I'll be thinking things aren't really so bad after all. It's as if all my negative thoughts turned into skin cells that got washed off by the blessed water.

By the time I got out of the shower, I had decided that Briana had probably lied about knowing Cupcake. They had never been delinquent kids together, never stolen things from people's houses. They probably hadn't even grown up in the same town. I sort of thought she might have been telling the truth about killing an uncle who had molested her, though. Her eyes had taken on a dull aching look when she'd told it that looked like she was remembering a true event. And if she'd killed somebody when she was still a teenager, she might find it easy to kill somebody now.

I patted myself dry, pulled a comb through my wet hair, shrugged on a terrycloth robe, and stuffed my damp towel in the washer with my clothes. I turned on the washer and joined Ella on my bed. I was asleep before the washer had begun its chugging.

I woke up a little chilled from the air conditioner set in the wall above my bed. I sat up and stretched, which made Ella sit up and open her mouth wide in a yawn. I jammed the wet laundry into the dryer and padded to the kitchen to make a cup of tea. Ella leaped daintily to the floor and followed me. My galley kitchen is separated from my living room by a one-person bar. The kitchen is so small I can stand in one spot and reach just about everything, which made it possible to fill a teakettle with water and drop a tea bag in a mug without thinking about it. Instead, I thought about Cupcake and Jancey and Briana and the murdered woman.

When the water boiled, I poured it over a tea bag. While it steeped, I stared at it as if I might find truths in the darkening water. I didn't. When I judged the color to be tea, I fished out the soggy bag and tossed it in the trash can under the sink, then ambled to my office-closet, where I conduct the bookkeeping part of my business. On the way, I flipped on the CD player and put on some nerve-soothing guitar by Segovia.

When my grandfather built the garage apartment, he was constrained by the existing boundaries of the carport, so it's understandable that the rooms would be small squares laid out in a straight line, with a narrow central hall where he put an alcove for the washer and dryer. But he must have miscalculated somehow and ended up with extra space he hadn't expected, because the closet is extravagantly roomy. A desk for record keeping sits on one wall, and the opposite wall is filled with shelves for my folded tees, shorts, jeans, underwear, and a few sweaters. My scanty collection of dresses and skirts hangs on the end wall across from a mirrored wall between two pocket doors.

I put my tea on the desk, and Ella jumped onto the desktop. She knows the routine as well as I do. Music plays, she bends the tip of her tail to the beat, and I return phone calls from clients, handle whatever business needs handling, and record my client visits.

I'm very meticulous about keeping records of my pet visits. I note every visit, what I did there, and anything out of the ordinary that I found. Usually that means something like a cat sneezing or a bird looking droopy on its perch, not a half-naked woman parading around in the homeowner's big shirt. Definitely not a woman with her throat slit. Nevertheless, I had to make some record of my visit to Cupcake Trillin's house, so I wrote: *Intruder present, called 911. Officers found homicide victim. Cats taken to Kitty Haven until house is clear for their return.*

I thought that covered the situation very nicely. Except for the part about the intruder having stalked Cupcake and him lying about knowing her.

When I finished the clerical duties, Segovia was still playing, and I couldn't find any excuse to kill more time. Feeling defensive before he even answered, I called Sergeant Owens. Even after being away from the department almost four years, I remembered his number by heart.

Caller ID told him it was me, so he was already ready for my question when he picked up his phone. Without even saying hello, he said, "The suspect turned herself in about an hour ago, Dixie. Came in with her attorney. I'm sure the investigating officer will want to talk to you, but it's just a formality."

He sounded defensive, too, as if he'd expected me to ask him why the heck his new homicide detective hadn't contacted me so he could follow the dots in tracing what had happened that morning. Guidry would have questioned me within minutes of arriving at the scene. Their new guy must be a lot slower.

It was at that moment that I should have said, "Oh, by the way, I just happen to have spent about an hour with the suspect before she turned herself in. She told me she's known Cupcake Trillin practically her whole life. I'm sure she's lying, because Cupcake wouldn't lie about knowing a famous model who's been stalking him. I mean, why would he?"

I didn't say that for a whole bunch of reasons, the main one being that even though I wasn't a deputy anymore, Owens would have my head on a platter if he knew I'd talked to Briana while officers were looking for her. Another big reason was that Cupcake was my friend, and I'm loyal to my friends, even when I have the teensiest suspicion one of them may have lied to me. Which, no matter how much I told myself it was Briana who had lied about knowing Cupcake, I sort of did.

So for those reasons plus a few more, I kept my mouth shut about seeing Briana and taking her to Ethan's office. Like a kid with sugar on her cheeks hoping nobody will guess she's been snitching cookies, I figured Briana might keep quiet about me and maybe nobody would ever know.

Instead, I said, "When will the investigators be done with the house? I'll need to call the crime-scene cleaners before I can take the cats back home."

Owens said, "Check with me in the morning and I'll know more about that. I've talked to Mr. Trillin. He and his wife will leave Parma for Rome a little after midnight our time. If they make all their connections, they'll get to Sarasota around ten tomorrow night. Twenty-one damn hours in the air."

I had never heard Owens profess so much interest in somebody's travel plans. He was trying to divert my attention from the investigation.

I said, "Who is the homicide detective on the case?"

Curtly, he said, "I'll know more about that tomorrow, too."

He clicked off without saying good-bye, which left me staring at my phone. Owens is never a gushy guy, but he's not rude. He didn't want to talk about the homicide detective on this case. Guidry had waited until the department had hired his replacement before he left, but this was going to be a high-profile case, and my bet was that the new guy hadn't worked out. The department was probably scrambling to find somebody with the experience to handle it.

I wished I knew if the murdered woman had been identified.

I wished I knew if Cupcake was lying about knowing Briana.

I wished I knew if Briana had told the truth about a mysterious person coming into the house and murdering the woman.

If Briana's story was true, a vicious killer was on the loose.

7

Before it was time to go on my afternoon calls, my cell phone rang with the distinctive ring reserved for Michael, Paco, or Guidry. My heart did the same little tap dance it always did when I heard that ring, because I hoped it was Guidry. Guidry had left Sarasota in November, and at first he had called often. After almost six months, not so much.

I hoped he'd got over his disappointment that I'd stayed in Siesta Key. I hoped he didn't miss me. I hoped he missed me and hurt every waking moment because I wasn't there.

I wished I would quit missing him.

I was a mess.

The call wasn't from Guidry. It was my brother, Michael.

He said, "I just heard a news report about a killing at Cupcake Trillin's house. Aren't you taking care of his cats?"

I gave him a quick rundown of what had happened, leaving out the part about talking to Briana and taking her to see Ethan Crane. Michael tends to get stressed when I get involved in things having to do with crime. He goes into burning buildings without the least hesitation, but murder investigations make him uneasy. Especially if I'm part of them.

He said, "The news report said the woman who did it turned herself in. Some big-name model, it sounded like."

"If that's what they're reporting, they've got it wrong. She turned herself in because she knew they were looking for her, but she says somebody came in while she was in another room and killed the woman. She may be telling the truth."

Michael's voice grew suspicious. "How do you know what she's saying?"

"I called Sergeant Owens."

It was absolutely true that I had called Owens, so technically I wasn't lying.

"According to the TV reporter, the judge denied bail for her because she broke into the Trillin house and because they think she was stalking Trillin. With her history, I guess they think she'll run if they let her out."

I didn't think there was any question that Briana would definitely *want* to leave if she thought she could hide out and never be found. But since her face was so famous, leaving wasn't really an option for her.

I was afraid I'd give away the fact that I knew Briana better than the TV reporter did if I talked to Michael any longer, so I told him I was on my way out the door for afternoon pet visits. I was *almost* on my way out, so it was only a small lie.

He said, "I'll be home in the morning. Love you."

"Love you."

We always end our conversations like that. Both of us have plenty of reason to know that every day might be our last, so we don't leave love unsaid.

I hurried to get dressed in my regulation khaki cargo shorts and sleeveless white tee. I slipped on fresh white Keds from the drying rack over the washer/dryer — I can't stand shoes that smell like feet, so I go through a lot of Keds. Then I called the guy who does homicide cleanup.

I said, "I wanted to give you a heads-up about a cleaning job in Hidden Shores. So far as I know, there's only one contaminated floor in one room. I'll let you know when the criminalists are done there."

"What kind of floor?"

"Tile."

"What kind of tile? May have to replace it."

"Expensive tile. The owners of the house are out of the country, but they'll be home tomorrow night. If you have to replace the tile, they can give you the particulars."

He thanked me for giving him a chance to plan ahead, and we said our good-byes. He didn't ask the homeowners' name, and I didn't volunteer the information. He was a professional, he knew not to pry.

Morning and afternoon, my first pet stop is at Tom Hale's condo on Midnight Pass Road. Tom is a CPA whose life went off on a different road than he'd intended when a wall of door displays fell on him at a home improvement store and crushed his spine. Life is like that. One moment you can be strolling down an aisle in a store admiring doorknobs, and the next moment you're not who you used to be but somebody totally different.

After his agony and fear and fury had got sorted out, Tom faced life as a paraplegic without a CPA office, a wife, or children. Well, he still had children, but his ex-wife had taken them and most of his settlement money to another state. But Tom's not one to sit around feeling sorry for himself, so he started over in a wheelchair. Instead of doing CPA work in a fancy office, he does it at his kitchen table. He adopted a greyhound racing dog, who had also been given up by the world as useless, and named him Billy Elliot.

Some retired greyhounds are happy to leave their racing days behind them, but not Billy Elliot. He needs a good twenty minutes of all-out running twice a day, so Tom and I do a trade-off. I run with Billy, and Tom handles my taxes and anything that has to do with money.

I took the mirrored elevator to Tom's floor, knocked lightly on his door to let him and Billy know I was there, and let myself in with my key. Tom yelled hello from the kitchen, and Billy met me in the foyer grinning and wagging his tail in absolute ecstasy. I love that about dogs. They don't stand back and make you work at being friends with them, they're your best friend the minute they see you.

I got Billy Elliot's leash from the closet and went to stand in the kitchen doorway. Tom had his laptop computer open on the table, and he looked up at me with a friendly grin. Not as friendly as Billy Elliot's, but friendly. If Tom were a dog, he'd be a standard poodle. He has short curly black hair, round black eyes, and a round face.

When he's working, he wears round glasses with black rims that make him look a little bit like a grown-up Harry Potter.

Tom's on his computer a lot. I suppose he researches things for business. Maybe he also e-mails and tweets and chats and blogs, I don't know. I'm the only person in the western hemisphere who doesn't do any of those things, and I don't ever intend to. But occasionally I need the kind of information that computer-savvy people can get in a trice — whatever a trice is — and when I do, I throw myself on Tom's mercy.

I said, "You know that football player named Cupcake Trillin?"

"I know somebody got killed in his house this morning."

Bad news really travels fast.

"I've just been wondering, you know, where he's from. Could you look that up?"

Tom gave me a calculating look, probably the way he scans a list of numbers when he suspects some of them are wrong. "He's from Louisiana."

Sports fans always know where sports stars came from. They may not know where their best friends grew up, but they know all the statistics about their favorite athletes.

"Yeah, but *where* in Louisiana? Like where did he go to high school?"

Flat voiced, Tom said, "You want to know where Cupcake Trillin went to high school."

"I just wondered."

"I don't mind looking it up, but you know him. Why don't you just ask him?"

Billy Elliot had come to sniff at the backs of my knees, a not-so-subtle reminder that he and I had some running to do.

I slapped Billy's leash against my open palm. "The Trillins won't be home until tomorrow night. You know how it is when you start wondering about something and you want to know *right then* or you'll never get it out of your mind. Like the name of a movie star that you can't remember."

Tom gave me a long hard look. He obviously thought I had some other reason for asking, but he was too polite to say so. "I'll do a search while you and Billy run."

Billy Elliot shoved his head against my thigh, and I bent and snapped his leash on his collar. Tom watched me the entire time. I could feel question marks pelting me, but I led Billy out of the apartment without giving Tom any excuses for wanting to know where Cupcake had gone to high school. I figured I'd take it one step at a time.

Tom's condo building has a parking lot with a green oval in the middle. Cars park around the perimeter of the oval, and the blacktop driving area makes a perfect track for Billy Elliot to pretend he's back chasing a mechanical rabbit while humans in the stands cheer and wave and slosh beer on one another. He's very considerate of the fact that I'm two-legged and therefore slow. On the first lap he takes it easy, or at least runs at a pace he considers easy. I gallop along behind him and try not to wheeze. But by the third or fourth lap he's decided that the blonde behind him has had plenty of warm-up time. He stretches his body out and goes for broke while I sort of leap and lurch to keep up with him. When we're done, he's grinning and whipping his tail in pure joy, and I'm a sweaty, red-faced, quivering blob.

On the way up in the mirrored elevator, I sagged against one wall and eyed my rumpled reflection. Even though Billy and I go through the same routine twice a day, I'm always impressed at the way he glories in the fact that he's designed for speed. The animal kingdom has its natural athletes the same way humans do. And, like humans, if they're not allowed to be what they were designed to be, they get depressed or mean.

At Tom's apartment, I hung Billy's leash on its hook in the foyer closet while Billy trotted to the kitchen to wag his tail at Tom by way of saying, "I had a really good time, Dad!"

I followed him, got a glass, filled it at the sink, and leaned on the counter while I drank it.

Tom tapped some keys on his computer to bring up a screen. "Cupcake Trillin's birth name was Alvin. He's from Thibodaux, Louisiana, which is the parish seat of Lafourche Parish. Has about fourteen thousand people and is about seventy-five miles southwest of New Orleans. Cupcake played for the Thibodaux High School Tigers and graduated in 2002. Got a sports scholarship to Tulane, played for the Green Wave, then signed with the Bucs right out of college."

"The Green Wave?"

Tom looked up with pity. "That's the Tulane football team."

"Oh."

I cleared my throat. "Uh, could you look up another name?"

Tom's round eyes became oval, as if he knew the other name was the one I really was interested in.

"What name?"

"Weiland." I spelled it for him.

"Got a first name?"

I cleared my throat again. It seemed to

have acquired a lump.

"Briana."

"As in the name of the model they say was in Cupcake Trillin's house when somebody was murdered? The one they're looking for?"

"She turned herself in. They're not looking for her anymore."

"Uh-huh."

"It would be in that town where Cupcake is from."

His fingers went into a holding pattern above the keys while he stared at me. "Are you saying they know each other?"

I erased the idea with the palm of my hand. "I just heard something about Briana being from that same town. I don't know if it's true. Even if it is, that doesn't mean they know each other."

Tom bent back to the computer keyboard but after a while shook his head.

"If I search for 'Briana,' I get a ton of articles. She was on the cover of *Vogue* and *Sports Illustrated.* Hung out with all the other big-name models. Looks like she's partied with every rock star in the world, too, not to mention some prime ministers and a few kings. But I don't find any mention of the name Weiland."

He clicked on a link, read some text, and

wrinkled his nose.

"She was tight with a Serbian gangster who was arrested for shipping heroin in a crate of counterfeit Gucci watches. He skipped off before his trial and went to a beach resort. Apparently hid out in plain sight for a long time. Took a false name, threw big parties for people like Briana, generally lived it up. Somebody tipped off the police and got a big reward. The guy got a four-year prison sentence, but another inmate killed him the first week."

Tom looked at me over the tops of his glasses. He looked a bit like the caterpillar in *Alice in Wonderland.* "This babe is a piece of work."

Briana hadn't struck me as a woman who held many ethical values of any kind, so I wasn't surprised that she had cozied up to a criminal. But my interests were a lot closer to home, like where Briana had grown up, and if she had known Cupcake when she was a kid.

I said, "I guess Briana's not from Louisiana, then."

"Wait, I'll check Louisiana birth records."

He tapped some more keys, leaned to read the screen, tapped more, wiggled the mouse thing more, and then shook his head.

I said, "So she lied."

“Not necessarily. Maybe her birth was recorded under a different name.”

“But if she were from Cupcake’s town, wouldn’t the name come up in some way?”

“Search engines only go to words that are registered somewhere or have been in the news or have a record of previous searches. If she got a reward for something like perfect school attendance in junior high, a search engine wouldn’t catch that.”

Which meant I didn’t know more than I had before. Briana had said she’d lied about where she’d come from, but maybe she’d lied about lying. The only way I would find out for sure if she’d really known Cupcake when they were kids was to ask him. And since it really wasn’t any of my business, I’d have to decide if there was good reason to tell him what Briana had told me. Good reason other than satisfying my curiosity and giving Cupcake a chance to prove to me that he wasn’t a liar.

I thanked Tom and left him looking suspicious and puzzled. I felt the same way, just not about myself.

Back on Midnight Pass Road, I headed north. My next client was about a mile away on the Gulf side, so I got into the left turning lane and waited for a break in traffic. A white Jag convertible with a male driver whizzed by in the southbound lane. The Jag was the same model as the Jag Briana drove.

Now here's the thing about having been a law enforcement officer. For the rest of your life, you notice the numbers on license plates. Some area of your brain registers them and retains them even when you don't consciously intend to. I could see the Jag's license plate in my rearview mirror, and the plate was the same as Briana's. The light changed, but instead of turning left, I made a U-turn and followed the Jag.

Call me nosy, but I wanted to know who was driving Briana's car.

8

So many tourists come to the Key that we locals are accustomed to driving behind cars that stop at every intersection while the drivers peer down a tree-lined lane that might or might not be the one they're looking for. But the driver of the Jag sailed on as if he was familiar with the terrain and knew exactly where he was going. Near the southern Bay side of the Key, the Jag whipped a fast left turn that sent shell dust flying from under his wheels. I followed him onto a lane where big estates and small villas kept company among palms and live oaks and sea grape. The Jag pulled into one of the curvy driveways leading to a stucco two-story, neither mansion nor modest villa. I drove straight ahead, watching the driver in my rearview mirror. He got out of the car, hurried in a measured trot to the front door, and opened it without knocking or ringing a bell.

I slowed the Bronco to a crawl and stopped at the curb. I felt stupid. What had I expected, that the driver would get out and hold up a sign for me that told me his name and his relationship with Briana? He had entered the house as if he lived there, which told me nothing. He had left Briana's car in the driveway, so he wasn't afraid he'd be caught out for driving it.

I sat and considered my options. I could call Ethan and ask him if he knew who had Briana's car, and why. But if I did that, Ethan would know that I was sticking my nose into a place where it definitely had no business being stuck. Besides, he might not know the answer. He had introduced Briana to her defense attorney, but that was his only involvement in the case. Unlike me, Ethan minded his own business.

The other option was that I could be like Ethan. I could drive away, take care of my pet clients, wait like the rest of the world to find out if Briana had killed the woman in Cupcake's house or if some phantom killer had come in the house while Briana was getting dressed. I could stop thinking about Briana's lies and secrets. I could stop thinking about Cupcake's lies and secrets. I could concentrate on my own lies and secrets.

A sharp tapping on my window made my

head jerk around so fast I heard my neck pop. A broad-faced woman with frizzy lavender hair was looking in at me with a smirky smile that said she found my presence rude and disrespectful and that she was looking forward to telling me so.

I stretched my lips in a pretend smile and lowered the window.

She said, "This is a private street. Are you lost?"

I said, "I'm, um, I'm looking for a lost cat."

Her gaze became a shade less haughty. A lost person didn't get her respect, but a lost cat did. "What kind of lost cat?"

My mind zipped to the place where big fat falsehoods live. There was a large yellow cat there.

"He's yellow. And white. Big. Longhair. Looks like a Dreamsicle."

For a second, her face fell at some secret disappointment. Then she waved her arm in an excited arc.

"Well, what do you know about that! He's in my house! I was going to run an ad about him! Come on in!"

That's the trouble with lying. Sometimes your lies rise up and smile at you and there's nothing you can do except take their hand and pretend you're friends.

Feeling like an idiot, I slunk out of the Bronco and followed the lavender-haired woman up her driveway to her villa. She was built like a sweet potato, with the retired Floridian woman's pull-on white knit pants and loose top. Her right foot must have been sore, because she tilted a bit to the left. With a genuinely nice smile, she held the front door open, and I dragged my own feet inside. It was a typical single retiree's villa: open floor plan with a bar separating the kitchen from the living area, lots of glass to let in the sun, creamy white tile floor, rattan furniture with creamy white linen cushions, creamy white walls hung with big splashy watercolors of sailboats on blue water under blue skies. A big white and yellow long-haired cat was draped over the top of a chair. He looked extremely contented.

A Pomeranian with electric white hair trotted to sniff my Keds.

The woman said, "Don't mind Snowball, she won't bite."

I smiled down at Snowball, who delicately licked my ankle.

The woman said, "The cat just showed up at my door a few days ago. I've been calling him Cecil. He looks like a Cecil, don't you think? He's a funny duck. He steals shiny things out of wastebaskets. Foil, or those lids on frozen dinners that are shiny on one side. I can't put a single shiny thing in the wastebasket anymore. I have to take it straight to the can in the garage."

She sounded proud of the cat's thievery.

She said, "I had a cat one time that lived to be twenty years old. I cried my eyes out when he died, just like if a child had died."

I nodded. "That's how it is when you love a pet."

With a yearning look at the cat, she said, "Where did you say this cat lives?"

The cat yawned and turned its head away from me.

I said, "You know what? This isn't the cat I'm looking for! The cat I'm looking for is a lot bigger and has more white in his coat."

"Oh, that's too bad!" Her eyes twinkled with delight.

I said, "I wonder if the people in that villa with the white Jaguar convertible in the driveway might have seen my cat. Do you know them?"

"Those French people? I doubt it. They're not permanent."

"They're French?"

She waved her hand. "They speak something foreign."

"Could they be Swiss?"

She was looking at me funny. "I don't

think I caught your name."

The question spooked me. I suddenly felt like a criminal about to be thrown in the slammer if I didn't come up with a cover name.

"Uh . . . it's Bridget. Bridget Jones."

Oh, Lord, I had given her the name of a movie! I was not only a total idiot, I was getting myself in deeper trouble with every lie I told.

I said, "I'm so sorry to take up your time! I'll just get out of your way and keep looking for the other cat."

"Well, if you're sure it's not the same cat."

"You know, I'll bet this cat chose to live with you. Cats do that, you know. If you haven't seen any lost-cat signs in the neighborhood, I think this cat was meant for you."

She looked hopeful. "You think?"

"I really do."

"I've missed having a cat. I love Snowball, but cats get to your heart in a different way, you know?"

I was already at the door, trying not to look like an escaping felon. "Thank you so much! Enjoy Cecil! 'Bye!"

With a nervous fake laugh, I skittered out and pulled the door closed behind me. I broke into an undignified lope down to the sidewalk, where a hibiscus hedge would hide me if she came out to ask where I'd come from. Sweaty with shame, guilt, and anxiety, I made it to the Bronco in record time and zoomed away.

In my imagination, I saw a TV reporter interviewing the sweet lavender-haired woman with the yellow cat and the white Pomeranian. The woman was saying, "I knew she was lying about looking for a lost cat. I asked her to come in so I could find out what she was doing in the neighborhood, and then she gave me that phony name. As soon as she left, I called the police and they arrested her."

At least I'd learned that the man driving Briana's car had recently moved to Siesta Key, and that he spoke a foreign language to another person who lived in the house with him. The woman with the Pomeranian had said "they" might be French, which could mean that more than two people lived there. Perhaps Briana lived in that house when she wasn't hanging out in Cupcake's house and wearing his shirt. Or perhaps the woman who'd been murdered in Cupcake's house lived there. I groaned. Maybe they all lived there. For all I knew, Briana was part of a Swiss ménage à trois, and I was a provincial fool doomed to live the rest of my life alone, not even smart enough to come up with a plausible fake name.

For the rest of the afternoon, I minded my own business. I walked an elderly boxer with creaky knees and sad eyes. I cleaned litter boxes. I groomed cats. I tossed a Frisbee for a hyperactive terrier, and I played chase-the-peacock-feather with a Russian Blue who could leap as high as my head. I brought in mail and left it neatly stacked on hall tables. I watered house plants and vacuumed cat hair. At every house, I checked timers to make sure lights and TVs would turn on and off at various times to fool would-be burglars. I changed TV programs for the pets, too. Most of them like the nature channels during the day, but they seem to prefer kid shows in the late afternoon and early evening. They're not too crazy about cop shows or romantic comedies.

While I switched channels at one house, I caught a local news report about the murder at Cupcake's house. With my thumb suspended over the remote, I stared at old footage of Briana sashaying down a runway in Milan or Rome or Paris, her pelvic bones leading her pale lithesome body, shoulders held in a classic slouch, all that red hair tumbled around her face. That image segued into footage of Cupcake suited up in his football gear, his dark face behind the helmet's grid looking ferocious and huge.

The TV voice said, "A bizarre case of fame stalking fame became even more bizarre today when an unidentified woman was found murdered in the home of Tampa Bay Buccaneer Cupcake Trillin. A spokesperson with the Sarasota County Sheriff's Department said that the internationally famous model Briana had broken into Trillin's Sarasota home before the murder occurred. Briana, who uses only the one name, has not been formally charged with homicide, but she is being held without bail pending a hearing. Trillin, who was in Italy when the murder occurred, is on his way home."

I said, "I guess the department isn't telling Briana's real name."

The three cats who were patiently waiting for me to bring up their favorite TV show turned their wide eyes at me, giving me that phony innocent look that cats do when all the time they're wiser than anybody.

Embarrassed, I zipped through the rest of the channels until I found the one with flying birds.

I left the cats raptly watching their TV screen. As I headed home, I realized that I had become so caught up in shock that I hadn't given much thought to the identity of the woman who'd been murdered. I'd given even less thought to the identity of the mystery person Briana claimed had been the killer.

I needed to get my priorities straight. By her own admission, Briana was a liar and a thief. If Cupcake said he didn't know Briana, then he didn't know her. Briana was not only a mentally ill woman who broke into people's houses and hung out with Serbian heroin dealers, she was a murderer. Furthermore, it was silly of me to feel sad about Briana. If I should be sad about anybody, it was the dead woman, not a spoiled, headline-seeking, lying killer.

I told myself that all the way home, and I almost convinced myself. But the question still buzzed in my head: *Why* had Briana stalked Cupcake? It couldn't have been simply because he was a famous person. She was even more famous than he, so fame couldn't have been the allure. She didn't seem like a big sports fan, either.

For the first time, I wondered if it had been Jancey who was being stalked, not Cupcake. Jancey was a beautiful, poised woman who didn't have to rely on paparazzi to assure her she was admired. Any woman would envy Jancey, especially a woman like Briana who'd had to fight for everything she had. Perhaps Briana had stalked the Trillins not because she coveted Cupcake but because she envied Jancey's life. Perhaps she had thought the murdered woman was Jancey, and in some hallucinatory madness had killed her so she could take her place.

As I waited for the light at Stickney Point, a motorcycle gang on pimped up Gold Wings roared over the drawbridge. The lead bike was a two-seater with an elderly couple wearing matching black leather jackets, helmets, and goggles. A Scottish terrier rode proudly in a carrier on the back. The terrier wore a helmet, jacket, and goggles like his humans. The group turned onto Midnight Pass Road and made a fast turn into the parking lot of Cap'n Curt's Crab and Oyster Bar.

Seeing those Gold Wing geezers having fun reminded me that the secret to happiness was to mind my own business. It was not my responsibility to answer any of the questions about Briana or the woman killed in the Trillins' house. I was a pet sitter coming home after a trying day, not a sociologist or an investigative reporter. Furthermore, I was a hungry pet sitter without a brother to feed her. Michael wouldn't be home from his firefighting shift until eight the next morning, so there wouldn't be a meal laid out waiting for me.

Michael is the family cook and the firehouse cook. Since he was four and I was two and our mother left us alone to go off on a weekend binge, he has fed me. When he was four, he fed me peanut butter and jelly. Now that he's thirty-four, he serves more sophisticated fare, but it's always with the firm conviction that it's his duty to make good food for his little sister — and for Paco and his fellow firefighters and anybody else who might want to eat.

When I rounded the last curve in the lane to my apartment and saw Paco's truck parked in its carport slot, I perked up. When I saw Paco's Harley also in the carport, I perked up even more. Paco is as helpless as I am when he's hungry, and unless he had a case to work that night, I could rely on him to join me for a restaurant meal.

Paco is Greek American, but his coloring makes it easy for him to pass as Middle Eastern or Latin American or anything in between. After my brother, he's my best friend in all the world. He's so smart that he's sometimes a little bit scary, plus he's what women mean when they say "tall, dark, and handsome." Women tend to get lustful around him, but he and Michael have been a couple for thirteen years and neither of them has any intention of ever not being together.

He and Ella were on the deck waiting for the sunset, Paco stretched in an Adirondack chair my grandfather built decades ago, Ella sitting on his chest. Paco's eyes had dark shadows under them, and his skin had the dried look of weariness. He wore rumpled shorts and a loose T-shirt, his bare feet cool on the redwood floor. Ella wore her usual red, white, and black blocks of color. Paco gave me a lazy grin of welcome, and Ella flicked the tip of her tail. I took another wooden chair and sighed with relief at being home.

With the easy intimacy of people who don't need to talk, Paco and I looked toward the ball of fire sliding down the curve of blue sky. A few wisps of white cloud drifted across its face, and an occasional brave bird made a V as it flew by, but otherwise the sun held center stage.

There's something almost supernatural about a sunset over the Gulf, something that makes the sun seem to swell and pulsate with growing intensity, sending out a higher energy to meet the energy of beings who turn to it as a source of life. A hush falls over the edge of the sea as the sun draws closer to it. Birds cease their crying, humans stop their chatter, even the surf hitting the sand seems to whisper.

Entranced, we sat in goldenrod light as the sun flirted with the sea, now languorous, sultry, heavy with desire, then bold and brassy with coming-at-you demand. A breathless moment like the instant between a shutter clicking and the image being recorded forever, and the rim of the sun touched the sea. Bold now, sun and sea reached for each other and the sun sank into the sea's depths, leaving a wake of gilded aurora.

A shimmering golden highway stretching to the shore faded into the sea, and the sky's last wisps of turquoise and violet dimmed and disappeared. The day was over. Evening had begun.

9

I heaved a heavy sigh and looked morosely at Paco. He looked as if his day had been as trying as mine.

I said, "What are you doing for dinner?"

He grinned. "Guess what I found in the refrigerator."

"If it wasn't Michael to cook for us, I don't care."

"Almost as good. He left dinner."

I sat up with new hope. "You're kidding."

"I swear to God. He left a note."

We both got up and surged through the kitchen door as if we were ancient sailors hearing the call of exotic sirens. The kitchen is the only room in the house that Michael and Paco modernized when they moved in. They replaced my grandmother's four-burner range with a shiny six-burner job with a grill down its middle. A counter separates the range from a column formed by three ovens set into the wall, and there are Sub-Zero things all over the place to keep all the stuff Michael stocks. If you're not paying attention in Michael's kitchen, you're liable to stick your hand in a drawer intending to grab a napkin and instead come up with a handful of lettuce leaves.

A butcher-block island with a salad sink at the far end runs down the center of the kitchen and serves as both dining table and workstation. Paco picked up a note from the island and waved it at me, then folded his arms and grinned while I read it:

Dear Big Doofus and Little Doofus,
Knowing that you may starve without me to feed you, I have left you a casserole and salad. Heat the oven to 425. Take the foil off the casserole. Put it in the heated oven for 15 to 20 minutes until it's bubbling and the top is slightly browned. Remove. Turn off oven. Love, Michael
PS: I'm assuming you know what to do with the salad.

I said, "Hot damn!"

"Amen."

I said, "I have to shower first."

"While you do that, I'll open the wine and turn on the oven."

"What did he make?"

"Who cares? It's food, and we don't have to go anywhere to get it."

I galloped off, charged up the stairs to my apartment, and within ten minutes was out of the shower and pulling on white gauzy pants and a bright yellow floating gauzy top with spaghetti straps. I love that gauzy stuff for lazy Florida nights. It's like being invisibly naked. I slid my feet into flip-flops, shoved a wide white abalone bracelet on one wrist, and thundered down the stairs.

Paco had set the butcher-block with big white plates, napkins, and tall wineglasses. A bottle of white wine chilled in an ice bucket. A big salad bowl sat in the middle of the butcher block. Paco looked extremely proud of himself. From her perch on her favorite bar stool, Ella looked proud of him, too.

Paco said, "I set the temperature, the thing dinged, so I already put the pan in the oven. I tossed the salad, too." Paco's one culinary expertise is that he makes a great olive oil and lemon juice salad dressing.

We high-fived.

I went to the wall of ovens and peered through the glass door of the top one. A square casserole dish sat on the rack.

"How much longer does it have to cook?"

"Uh, I think it's been in around five minutes."

"You didn't set the timer?"

He looked uncertain. "He didn't mention setting a timer."

Paco goes out every day disguised as a criminal of the worst kind. He infiltrates gangs and wrestles killers to the ground. He's a tough, experienced cop, and other tough, experienced cops trust him with their lives. But when it comes to heating a casserole in an oven, he has to have written instructions.

I said, "That's okay, we'll just watch for it to bubble and turn brown. What is it?"

He shrugged. "I only know there's grated cheese on top."

I smiled thanks at him. I just hate it when somebody knows something before I do.

While we waited for the cheese to bubble, Paco opened the wine and splashed some in two glasses. I made note of the fact that he was having wine for dinner because it meant he wasn't on duty that night. In his line of work, Paco's life depends on keeping a clear head and quick reflexes, so he's scrupulous about avoiding alcohol before going off to deal with the scum of the world. I didn't mention it though. When you love somebody whose everyday duties could kill them, you don't let them see that you worry about them. You just quietly pay attention to tiny details, like fatigue shadows under their eyes and the fact that they drink wine with dinner instead of water or tea.

When we judged the cheese on the casserole sufficiently bubbling and brown, Paco manfully pulled on a pair of Michael's oven mitts and rescued the pan from the oven. I leaped to put a trivet on the butcher block, and he set the casserole down with a triumphant flourish.

I said, "Yaaay!"

Ella waved her tail and gazed at Paco with undisguised adoration.

He switched the oven control to OFF, and we both took seats at the island.

Paco picked up a big serving spoon and approached the casserole like a bomb-squad cop getting ready to inspect a ticking package. He plopped big servings on each of our plates, and we both leaned over them and said, "Mmmm."

Michael probably should have left instructions on how to dish it up, because it turned out to be seafood crepes under a creamy, cheesy, white sauce, and the crepes didn't end up intact on our plates. I doubt that Paco noticed that, and I didn't care. It was a perfect dinner for two people worn out by honest work that put them up against some people whose work was far from honest.

For several minutes, we didn't make any sounds except moans of appreciation. Then Paco got a second helping and looked at me with renewed energy.

He said, "I know what happened today at Trillin's house."

That didn't surprise me. More than likely, every deputy in Sarasota County knew all the particulars about the murdered woman in Cupcake's house, just like everybody in town knew that a famous model named Briana had been there.

I scraped the last bite from my plate and took a sip of wine. "What you don't know is that Briana followed me when I left. She wanted to talk to me, asked for my help. I don't know if I did the right thing or not, but I met with her at the beach pavilion, and I led her to Ethan's office. He took her to the defense attorney who went with her to turn herself in."

Paco's gaze was steady. If Michael had been home, he would have had steam coming from his ears when he heard what I'd done. Paco is calmer. Not less protective of me, just calmer about it.

He said, "Did she kill the woman?"

"She says she didn't, but her story is weak.

She claims she went to change her clothes after I left — which really means put on some clothes, because she was damn near naked when I went in Cupcake's house to take care of the cats. She says when she went back to the living room the woman was on the floor dead. She says she doesn't know who the woman was, doesn't know who came in and killed her."

"The investigating team said the security company has no record of her entering or leaving the front gate or the house."

So Paco not only knew what had happened at Cupcake's house, he knew some inside details. I let that slide without comment, but I noted it because Paco is a special investigator, not a homicide detective.

I said, "If Briana is telling the truth, she's an accomplished thief. She told me she has an electronic gizmo that disables security systems for the few seconds it takes to go through them. Her story is that she left the house, climbed a ladder she'd conveniently hidden in those vines on the walls around Hidden Shores, got in her Jaguar parked out of sight on the other side, and waited until she saw me drive through the security gates."

Paco sat for a moment without speaking,

his dark eyes staring at nothing. I knew he was imagining what I'd described, processing it, and comparing its plausibility against what he knew of available technology.

"She's saying she went in Trillin's house to rob it?"

I pinched the stem of my wineglass, shifting it a fraction of an inch to and fro on the butcher block while a contest went on between my loyalty to my friend Cupcake and my trust in Paco's wisdom and discretion.

"She says she just wanted to get close to him."

"Creepy."

"Paco, there's something really weird about the connection between Cupcake and Briana. He claims he never heard of her, but she told me she and Cupcake grew up in the same little town outside New Orleans. She said they were both poor and broke into houses to steal minor things they sold. She says she ran away from home when she was sixteen after she killed an uncle who'd been molesting her."

Paco's face wore the expression of somebody who had heard every story in the world and only believed half of them.

I said, "She told a different story to Ethan, the same line she gives the press about being from Switzerland."

"Which one of those stories do you believe?"

I said, "I don't know what to believe. I asked Tom Hale to look up Cupcake on the computer. He did go to school in a little town near New Orleans. He got a football scholarship to Tulane and then went pro. Tom didn't find records of Briana in the same town, but she could be telling the truth. But why would Cupcake lie about knowing her?"

"That's easy. The press loves to pile on a sports hero who turns out to have clay feet. Cupcake Trillin is known for being an honest guy who does a lot of philanthropic work to benefit poor kids. If he went public about being a delinquent kid who broke into people's houses with a girl who killed a man and then went on to be an internationally famous model, he'd either be made an idealized example of a bad kid who turned himself around, or he'd be roasted on a spit as a hypocrite. In either case, his face would be on every tabloid in the country. His entire past, his family, his friends, his every move would be scrutinized and posted on all the voyeur Internet sites."

"Voyeur sites?"

He smiled tightly. "We used to call people

who had an unhealthy interest in other people's private business window-peepers. Now we call them social networkers. If they got a hint that Cupcake Trillin had a past with the supermodel named Briana, they'd dig into it with long spoons."

"If he lied, he lied to his wife, too."

"The best lies are consistent."

"When she finds out, she'll be hurt."

"That's not your problem, Dixie. And if you're feeling hurt yourself because he lied to you, get over it. The man has to protect himself. Just because you're friends doesn't mean that he owes you absolute honesty about his entire life."

He sounded so emphatic that I wondered if Paco had some secrets himself. Maybe everybody does.

He said, "While you were in Trillin's house this morning, did you notice anything out of place? Anything that looked disturbed?"

He saw my surprise at the question and shook his head as if he were reprimanding himself. "Never mind."

When an undercover cop who knows more than he's supposed to know about a murder investigation asks you a direct question and then says, "Never mind," you mind plenty. You wonder what the heck he really wants to know.

He said, "On a scale of one to ten, with ten being the highest level of trust, how much credence do you give to Briana's claim that she didn't know the murdered woman?"

I took a deep breath and thought of the way Briana's voice had sounded, how her eyes had shifted as she talked. "I'd give it a four."

"How about the claim that she didn't know who came in and killed the woman?"

"I'd give that a two."

"Do you think she did the killing herself?"

"I didn't at first because the killer would have had to be taller than Briana to slit a woman's throat from behind. But as Ethan Crane pointed out the woman could have been knocked unconscious and lying on the floor when she was killed."

I waited for Paco to tell me what the coroner's report had been, because I was sure he knew. But he grasped the stem of his wineglass much the same way I had pinched mine, and studied the glass while he tilted the contents side to side.

He said, "This is bad business, Dixie. Stay out of it. You've done your civic duty by getting Briana to turn herself in. That was good of you. Now drop it."

Something about his voice caused a little

round ball to drop into a perfectly sized hole in my brain, like those puzzle games Michael and I played on long car trips when we were kids. If you tilted the boards exactly right, you could get every metal ball to settle into a hole. As if I had inadvertently tilted a puzzle board, I knew that Paco had information about the killing at Cupcake's house that turned the homicide into a case of far greater import than a murder.

With his skill at disguise, Paco had got close to underworld kingpins, infiltrated treacherous white-supremacist groups, Middle Eastern terrorist groups, and local theft rings. Something about the murder in Cupcake's house was important enough to bring Paco into its investigation. I didn't believe it was because Cupcake was a famous football player or because Briana was a famous supermodel. The importance had to do with the identity of the murdered woman, and that was something Paco knew and was keeping to himself.

We had crossed some invisible line, and we both immediately drew back from it. I said something to lighten the mood, Paco laughed, and we got up and busied ourselves rinsing dishes, loading the dishwasher, putting away leftovers, all the homely things people do to ignore the elephant in the room.

Ella sat on her bar stool and observed us like a queen watching her subjects. When the kitchen was tidied up, I stretched to kiss Paco's cheek, then bent to kiss the top of Ella's head.

I said, "Thanks, Paco."

"You're welcome."

He knew I wasn't thanking him for dinner. I was thanking him for listening to my secret about talking to Briana. I knew he wouldn't repeat it, not even to Michael. I was also thanking him for his advice about staying out of the murder investigation. It was good advice, and I intended to follow it. Mostly.

I went upstairs to my apartment wondering why the identity of a murdered woman would be kept a secret from the press. And why Paco would be involved in the investigation of the murder. I worried the idea for the rest of the evening, but when I fell asleep I was no closer to knowing the answer.

I dreamed that Cupcake and I went to a fancy restaurant where a sign was posted reading NO RANCOR. All the diners cut their eyes at it and tried to interpret its meaning without appearing ignorant. Cupcake finally braved the scorn of a haughty waiter and came right out and asked what the sign meant.

The waiter looked down his nose at him. "It means we're out of rancor."

Cupcake blinked. "Oh."

The waiter went away, and I whispered, "What is rancor?"

"Some kind of salad green, I think. Grows wild."

I said, "Oh yeah. I think my grandmother made rancor salad with chopped eggs and bacon. It had a bitter aftertaste."

The waiter returned, and I said, "Tell me, is rancor a seasonal dish?"

The waiter sniffed. "We use hothouse rancor. It's always in season, but our chef failed to get a supply today."

Cupcake said, "What do you have in its place?"

He sneered, "Nothing takes the place of true rancor, sir."

10

My alarm went off at 4:00 A.M. the next morning, and I swam up from sleep trailing remnants of my dream. On my way to the bathroom, my thoughts shot to Briana on a narrow bunk in a jail cell. Splashing water on my face and twisting my hair into a ponytail, I wondered if Briana was awake, too. I imagined her pacing her cell or huddled on the floor in despair. While I got into cargo shorts and a tank top and fresh Keds, I imagined a cellmate who hated Briana because she was a raving beauty and plotted to scratch her eyes out. Outside on my porch, I decided I suffered from an overactive imagination. Besides, as Paco had pointed out, Briana wasn't my problem.

I stopped for a minute to fill my lungs with the sea's salty breath and get my bearings. It was my favorite time of day — that tentative period while the moon and stars negotiate with the sun, and the universe waits to see if the night's rulers will gracefully exit and let a new day begin. A dull corrugated sea stretched toward a blurred horizon. On its surface, the reflection of retreating stars made winking lights like dying fireflies. Above it, a few desultory seabirds floated on high air currents. On the shore, a sleepy surf pretended to have every intention of getting its act together and making a bigger splash, but not just yet. I felt the same way.

Trailing my fingers on a stair railing damp with predawn dew, I went to the carport, where a trio of snowy egrets slept on the hood of my Bronco and a white pelican dozed on the roof. The pelican stretched his wings and smoothly sailed away when I opened the car door, but the egrets stayed put until I started the engine and their roosting place began to hum and vibrate. Even then they didn't seem put out about having to move, they just politely flew away. Egrets are friendly optimists.

As always, I stopped first at Tom Hale's condo, where Billy Elliot was aquiver with excitement in the dark foyer. I used my key, whispered a quick hello to him, got his leash from the foyer closet, and we were out the door in seconds, Billy's tail like a helicopter rotor of anticipation. He feels about his morning run the way caffeine addicts feel about their first cup of coffee.

At that hour, Billy and I pretty much had the parking lot's oval track to ourselves. The only other dog was an overweight basset hound leading an equally overweight man who wore pull-on knee supports on each leg and listed side to side like a ship in an uneven sea. Billy and I sped past man and hound. I nodded and smiled at them in a friendly good-morning way, but Billy's grin had a more disdainful look.

Tom was still asleep when Billy and I went back upstairs. Billy was calm and happy, I was still panting a little bit. I replaced his leash in the foyer closet, smooched the top of his head, and left him looking like a pampered athlete who knew his trainer would soon appear with a postexercise serving of protein.

The rest of my morning calls went smoothly. I walked a fluffy white bichon frise whose human had broken an ankle by stepping in the pool skimmer while she was emptying the basket. The bichon was polite during our walk but eager to return to her human. I fed and walked two miniature dachshunds whose human had gone to Orlando for the day. They were also polite but kept giving each other raised eyebrows because I didn't do things exactly the way their human did them. I fed and cleaned the cage of a parakeet whose human was out of town for a week. The parakeet was muttering to itself when I left, and I had a feeling it was counting the hours until its human would return. I didn't take it personally. We all like things to stay the same.

The rest of my calls were to cats, all of whom pretended not to miss their humans one iota. Cats are like that. I think it's because they give their hearts so completely to their humans that they feel embarrassed about it. To cover the fact that they're more sentimental than the gooiest Hallmark card, they put on a big show of indifference.

Most of the morning's cat clients remembered me from earlier times, so they tolerated me without fearing they'd been abandoned by the ones they loved. The new ones accepted my food and my grooming with wary appreciation. It takes a cat a while to trust a new person. I'm that way myself, so I don't take offense.

Midway through the morning, Sergeant Owens called to give me the go-ahead on having the crime-scene cleaners go to the Trillins' house.

I said, "Do you have an identification for the murdered woman yet?"

He said, “As I recall you’re usually at the Village Diner around ten o’clock.”

I hate it when people answer a question with another implied question. Besides, I didn’t like him implying that I was the kind of person whose routine was so rigid that the entire sheriff’s department knew it. But like it or not, I had to agree that I could usually be found slurping coffee every morning at the Village Diner around ten.

He said, “An investigator working on the homicide will probably stop by while you’re there. He wants to talk to you about what you saw yesterday.”

“Your new homicide detective?”

Owns cleared his throat, mumbled something to somebody else, and said, “Gotta go, Dixie.”

He clicked off and left me with the uneasy awareness that he had avoided answering both my questions. Owens wasn’t the kind of man to get touchy about a delay in identifying a homicide victim. Furthermore, I doubted that Owens would be uncomfortable talking to me about the detective who had replaced Guidry. Which meant that what I’d suspected was true. The department knew who the woman was, but they had some reason for not releasing the information.

But when I considered all the international attention the murder had attracted, I could understand why the sheriff's department might be reluctant to share details with the world. Especially if they were afraid their new homicide detective wasn't up to the job.

I called the crime-scene cleanup guy, who said the timing was great because his team could start work immediately.

I said, "When can the owners come home?"

"Depends on whether we have to replace the tile. If the tile's not contaminated, they *could* come back tonight. If it was me, I'd wait until tomorrow morning to let the odor of ozone and germicide spray dissipate."

"They have cats."

"Cats for sure will hate the smell. And, like I said, I won't know until I see it if we'll have to replace the tile. Check with me this afternoon and I'll be able to tell you more."

My next call was to the Ritz-Carlton, where I booked a suite for Cupcake and Jancey. Making hotel reservations for clients isn't my job as a pet sitter, but in this case I did it for the same reason I'd taken Elvis and Lucy to the Kitty Haven — I knew Cupcake and Jancey were too shocked and stressed to make arrangements for themselves.

At about nine forty-five, I pulled my Bronco into the Village Diner's parking strip. None of the other cars there looked like the unmarked sedans driven by Sarasota County detectives. Inside the diner, I waved to Judy, the waitress who's been there forever, and headed for the ladies' room. I knew Judy would alert Tanisha, the diner's cook, that I was there, and that Tanisha would get on my regular order and have it ready by the time I took a seat in my regular booth. Like I said, I'm so predictable it's downright pathetic.

I took a little extra time in the ladies' room. In addition to washing off all noticeable cat hair, I splashed water on my face, combed my hair, and redid the ponytail. I slicked on lip gloss, too, and eyed myself with extra care to make sure I looked presentable. I looked okay. With my Scandinavian ancestors, I have a kind of blue-eyed, blond, Jennifer-Aniston-girl-next-door-look. Not a raving beauty, but okay.

Judy had already poured a mug of coffee for me, and she set my breakfast down as I slid into my booth. Judy is tall and angular, with hazel eyes that hide hurt under defiance. She's one of my best friends, but we never go to movies or talk on the phone or do any of the things most friends do. Instead, we give each other little bits of gossip and an occasional intimacy at the diner. I know all about the good-for-nothing men who've taken advantage of her over the years, and she knows about Todd and Christy dying and about Guidry leaving. Judy thought I was an idiot for letting Guidry leave without me, and she thought it was her duty as a friend to point out my idiocy every chance she got.

She said, "Missed you yesterday."

I said, "Yeah, I had to be somewhere else."

She waited for more, but I just gave her a big smile.

I said, "Just so you won't think I'm having a wild love life if you see me with a man, I'm supposed to meet a detective here this morning."

She raised an eyebrow. "You getting mixed up in another murder?"

I shook my head. "It's just a formality. I was in the neighborhood. That kind of thing."

"Uh-huh. Well, I'll watch, and if a cop comes in, I'll send him to you."

She swayed her hips more than necessary as she walked away, sort of telling me she thought a wild love life would be better than an in-the-neighborhood kind of talk with a new detective.

Almost every day of my life, I have the same breakfast — two eggs over easy, extra-crispy home fries, and a biscuit. Tanisha does the best biscuits in the world. I was buttering my biscuit when Ethan Crane walked in the diner door. With his tall, wide-shouldered body in a dark pinstripe suit, stark black hair brushing the collar of a pale lavender shirt, he could have been on the cover of a romance novel. Maybe it was just because I liked to believe it was so, but the way his dark eyebrows rose in surprise when he saw me looked phony, the way people pretend to be surprised when friends jump out and yell, "Surprise!" when they've known all along that a surprise party was planned for them.

The estrogen level in the diner rose like fog as he walked toward me. My knife slipped so I sort of buttered my thumb instead of my biscuit. A woman across the aisle froze with her mouth open and her fork poised in midair with cheese grits dripping off it. Behind his back, Judy fanned herself with a menu.

Ethan has that effect on women.

He said, "Can I join you?"

Trying very hard to be cool, I gestured

with my buttery hand toward the booth seat. "Of course."

He slid into the booth, and Judy was beside him in an instant with a mug and coffeepot. If he'd asked, she would have run to the kitchen and brewed up a fresh batch that instant.

He said, "I'll have my regular."

Judy shot me a smug smile that said she knew what his regular was and I didn't.

I said, "I didn't know you came here often."

"Every day. But usually a lot earlier."

"Oh."

I wondered if I was the reason he had come later that day. Had he known that my schedule brought me there around ten, and purposefully delayed his own breakfast so it coincided with mine?

He said, "Talked to any wanted criminals today?"

"That was nice of you to get her an attorney. I understand she turned herself in."

"How do you manage to get involved with people like her? Do you have some kind of magnet?"

Judy skidded to his side and put down his breakfast. Tanisha is fast, but not that fast. Judy must have stolen an order intended for somebody else. Scrambled eggs, sliced tomatoes, unbuttered rye toast. The white smile he gave her sent her into a near swoon that she covered by topping his coffee.

I watched him cut into a tomato slice. He ate in the European way, both hands working knife and fork, fork tines turned down, spearing a bite of tomato and sort of stacking egg on the back of his fork before lifting it to his mouth. If I ate like that, I'd probably stab myself in the eye.

I said, "I don't *try* to attract people like Briana. It just happens. She was in the Trillins' house when I went in to take care of their cats, and then she followed me."

"You didn't have to talk to her."

I shoveled up some of my own egg in the American way. I speared a bite of fried potato. I chewed, I swallowed. He waited.

"I felt sorry for her."

His eyes were like dark pools of double chocolate fudge, warm enough to bathe nude in.

He said, "I hear that Guidry left."

I had an almost irresistible urge to make it clear that Guidry hadn't left *me,* he'd just left Sarasota.

"He was offered a job in New Orleans that he couldn't refuse."

Ethan nodded. His long fingers broke a triangle of rye toast in half and left both halves on his plate.

"Are you going to follow him?"

I swallowed. I hated that question.

"No."

"Why not?"

"It's hard to explain. You know how sometimes you know something is wrong for you even if everything about it seems right? I just knew I couldn't leave my home."

He leaned back in the booth. "That's why I'm here. I practiced law for a while in Colorado, but the white sand and the seabirds of Florida kept calling to me. When my grandfather died and left me his practice, I didn't think twice about it. This is where I belong."

"Do you miss anybody in Colorado?"

"Sure. Friends, colleagues. A woman."

"Ah."

"She felt the same way about mountains and snow that I felt about surf and sea."

"But now you're with somebody else."

"I was, but that didn't work out."

"I'm sorry."

That was *such* a lie!

I was glad it hadn't worked out, but I felt guilty because I was glad. Anyway, the fact that he was free didn't mean anything would happen between us.

He said, "Dixie —"

Before he could finish what he planned to say, I saw the new detective come into the diner. I knew he was a cop the minute I saw him, and probably half the other people in the diner knew it, too. Cops have an alert, watchful look, as if they can swivel their eyeballs and see through the backs of their skulls. The cop standing at the front of the diner scanning the booths also had the spine and shoulders of a career military man, that easy erectness that comes from vertebrae getting the habit of stacking themselves with the least effort.

I said, "Uh-oh, here's the new homicide detective who took Guidry's place. I'm supposed to meet him here."

Ethan turned to look at the man. "I'll leave you to it, then."

I could have offered to introduce them, but it would have been awkward for all of us. The homicide cop was there as part of an investigation into a murder that Briana might have committed, and Ethan had found a defense attorney for her.

Owens must have given him a description of me, because he started toward me as Ethan left. The two men met in the aisle and gave each other the dismissive once-overs that men do. The homicide guy was lean but not skinny, and I judged him to be midforties. He had that two-day-old beard thing going, along with dark shades and a thin leather bomber jacket. Dark hair cut short and growing gray, skin that was acquainted with sunshine but didn't live in it. Firm mouth that probably had to remind itself to smile.

He stopped beside my booth and gave me a curt nod. "Ms. Hemingway?"

"That's me."

I flipped my palm toward the other side of the booth in an invitation to sit, and he slid into the bench seat opposite me. Judy was instantly at his side to gather up Ethan's plate and mug.

"Coffee, sir?"

"Please."

We waited until she wiped off the tabletop and returned with a mug and coffeepot.

Without asking, she topped mine off, too.

The cop said, "Nothing else for me, thanks."

Judy gave him a megawatt smile, knocking herself out to be charming to the new cop in town, then went away still doing that extra hip-swinging thing.

He said, "My name is Steven." He said his name with a hint of an accent, almost *Stefan.*

He removed his dark glasses and looked gravely at me. He had green eyes, which somehow surprised me. You don't often see truly green eyes. I wondered if he wore colored contacts.

It's unusual for a law enforcement officer to invite witnesses to get chummy, but I had been so intrigued by his eyes and the way he pronounced his name that I didn't notice he hadn't shown me any creds. I just sat there with greasy steam rising from my fries and made nice with Sarasota's new homicide detective who had probably been born in some other country and who'd sort of been introduced to me by Sergeant Owens. I even felt a bit bountiful about it, the native putting the newbie at ease. If I noticed that his voice had an edge of agate hardness, I put it down to the fact that he was, after all, a homicide detective.

He said, "Why don't you just tell me what happened yesterday. All of it."

I was so nervous about my secret meeting with Briana that I talked like somebody hacking at brush with a machete, slashing words right and left, telling him every detail of what I had done at the Trillin house, what Briana had said, what Cupcake had said when I called, going on nonstop and hoping he would be so impressed with all the facts

I gave him that he wouldn't ask what had happened between me and Briana after I left the Trillins' house.

When I finished the part about taking Elvis and Lucy to the Kitty Haven, he nodded gravely and stayed quiet. Judy swished by to take my empty plate and refill our coffee mugs.

Steven said, "Now tell me the rest."

"That's it."

He made a slicing motion with the edge of his palm, and I stopped with an unspoken word still hanging on my bottom lip.

"Ms. Hemingway, cut the crap. We know you were in contact with Briana, and in case you don't know it, that makes you an accessory to a crime."

My mind was still so caught up in the power of words that it trotted after the word "accessory." I had been reduced to something like a handbag or a belt. A scarf, maybe, an accessory to smarten up something plain and dowdy. But I knew he didn't mean that kind of accessory. He meant the kind that can cause you to end up doing jail time.

My face went hot, and I took a sip of coffee to stall for time. "She was following me in traffic, and at a red light she ran to my car and asked if she could talk to me. I told her to meet me at the pavilion."

"Where you provided her with breakfast."

I tried to smile fetchingly. "Wow, you've done your homework!"

He didn't return the smile. "Tell me what the woman said to you."

"She said she didn't kill the woman. She said she went to the bedroom to get dressed and the woman was dead on the living room floor when she came out."

"What else did she tell you?"

I swallowed. I knew enough about criminal investigations to know that sometimes a detail that seems completely unrelated can be the key to solving a crime. But I also knew that telling this cop that Briana claimed to be an old friend of Cupcake's would put Cupcake in an untenable position. Cupcake's reputation and career could be ruined if cops started checking Briana's story, and I was almost positive she had lied.

I said, "This is something nobody knows. I'm embarrassed to tell it, but it may be important."

He waited, and it seemed to me that a light sparked in his dark eyes.

"I know where Briana lives. She leases a house in Oleander Acres."

His eyes never seemed to blink.

He said, "How do you know that?"

"Well, that's the embarrassing part. I saw her car on the street, and I followed it. She drives a white Jag convertible, and I saw it go by. A man was driving it. He went to a house, and I stopped across the street to look at the house. A neighbor came out to see why I was loitering there — it's a private street, and I guess they're careful about strangers — and she told me that some French people live in the house. Briana's from Switzerland, you know. I think they speak French."

He still hadn't blinked. "Ms. Hemingway, if you have any information about this case that you've held back, this is the time to tell me."

My head shake was more like an attack of palsy than denial. "I'm sure you already know that I led Briana to an attorney. Not a defense attorney, but an attorney who's a friend of mine. He contacted a defense attorney for her."

I heard myself babbling and prayed that I would shut up soon.

I said, "That's the last I saw of her. Sergeant Owens said the defense attorney went with her when she turned herself in."

I thought that was clever of me, to bring Owens into the conversation. Sort of like reminding this guy that I was one of the good guys, a former deputy, a woman on his side of the law.

He gazed at me a moment longer, then slid from the booth and stood up.

He said, "I'll talk to you again."

He walked down the aisle of booths, put down money at the cashier stand, and went out the door.

Judy came and stood beside me, watching through the glass door as he walked away.

She said, "You think you and that new cop are going to be as compatible as you were with the hunk?"

By "the hunk" she meant Guidry. She had a malicious grin and an even more malicious glint in her eyes.

I said, "That guy probably wasn't compatible with his own mother. Not even in the womb."

I didn't add that the man I'd just talked to might be Guidry's replacement, but he had a cold hardness that Guidry had never had. Guidry was tough, and when it came to getting facts he was unrelenting. But he had never looked at me with the unsympathetic eyes that Steven had. It gave me a bad taste in the mouth to consider how men like Steven dealt with people who withheld information from them.

11

I went out and sat in the Bronco and gave myself a good talking-to. I told myself that I was a citizen, and that I had a duty as a citizen to tell anything I knew that might help law enforcement agencies find the person who had killed a woman in Cupcake Trillin's house while Briana was there.

I rebutted that Cupcake Trillin had been in Italy with his wife when the murder happened, and that he'd had absolutely nothing to do with it. Whether he had or had not known Briana when he was a kid was an extraneous detail that would not shed light on the identity of the killer.

I counterargued that it was important only because he claimed Briana was a complete stranger and that he had no idea why she had been stalking him. If that was a lie, then it could be a vital piece of information.

I snarled that Cupcake was on a plane somewhere over the Atlantic and wouldn't be home until late that night. I could ask him for the truth when he came home, but in the meantime I had no way of finding out if he'd lied. Furthermore, if I told the investigators what Briana had told me, they would assume there was some nefarious connection between them, and they would be at the airport waiting for Cupcake when he got off the plane. Every reporter in town would already be there, and if they saw officers of the law meeting Cupcake, they would splash it all over the place. And, as Paco had said, no matter what the truth was, Cupcake's reputation, his marriage, and his career could be seriously damaged by that kind of negative publicity.

I started the Bronco and backed out of my parking place. I wasn't going to get in touch with the investigators and tell them what Briana had told me, but I didn't feel good about it.

I needed advice. I knew Michael had been home since eight that morning, but I also knew what his advice would be: stay out of it, mind my own business, cooperate with the law. I needed advice from somebody who cared about me but could be objective. Somebody like Reba Chandler.

Reba is a retired psychology professor with an African grey parrot named Big Bubba that I sometimes take care of. Big Bubba is one of the smartest birds in the world, most likely because his human is one of the smartest women in the world. Bubba is arrogant about it, but Reba hides her smarts under a calm friendliness. You only know she's way ahead of you when you try to feed her a line of baloney. She'll nail you every time.

I found her and Big Bubba on their lanai. Big Bubba was in his cage slinging seed hulls through the bars and muttering to himself, and Reba was on a chaise with her feet up, a book in her lap, and a tall glass of iced tea on the table beside her. When I tapped on the screen door, she and Big Bubba raised their heads as if I were a welcome distraction. Big Bubba flapped his wings and squawked, and Reba put her book aside and offered me iced tea. I declined the tea, went to Big Bubba's cage to give him a proper greeting, and then took a chair beside Reba.

She said, "I hear you were at the house where a murder happened."

That's Reba for you, she doesn't circle around things.

I said, "I guess it's all over the news."

"Well, not *you* so much, but the model and the football player."

I said, "Briana and Cupcake Trillin. I wanted to talk to you about them."

"Yes?"

That *Yes?* is how shrinks open the door wide enough for you to drive through with a truckload of stuff you wouldn't let anybody else see. She tilted her head a bit when she said it, a gesture she'd used with me since I was in high school. I had taken care of Big Bubba then, too, and gradually came to tell Reba every secret I had. She may be the reason I ended up with enough core strength to snap back to sanity after Todd and Christy were killed and I went seriously nuts.

I didn't tell her the investigation into the murder had taken a weird turn. That was law enforcement business, a line I wouldn't cross even with Reba. But the personal stuff was fair game. Personal stuff as in my own confusion about the story Briana had told about her history with Cupcake.

I said, "Briana's official story is that she's from Switzerland, and that her parents were killed in an accident when she was a child. Then a nice American couple adopted her and took her to a remote rural area in Minnesota where they home-schooled her. In other words, no school records, no neighbors to remember. She used to refuse to give her last name to avoid embarrassing those alleged adoptive parents, but now she says they've died."

Reba listened closely. Big Bubba had stopped muttering to himself, and I felt as if he was listening, too.

I said, "I won't go into how it happened, but yesterday I met with Briana at the beach pavilion, and she told an entirely different story. She said she was from the same little Louisiana town as Cupcake Trillin, and that they had been good friends when they were kids. Not ordinary good friends, but kids that broke into houses together and stole things. Petty stuff, but enough to sell for cash. She says she left there when she was sixteen, and that she's never seen Cupcake again. Except when she stalked him."

I leaned back in my chair. That was it. That was all I could tell. And I sounded like an idiot for telling it.

Reba said, "You don't like being lied to."

For some stupid reason, my eyes smarted as if tears were trying to break through.

I said, "I'm just trying to understand why a woman who became internationally famous would be stupid enough to stalk a man and break into his house."

"Sounds like the woman is determined to undermine her own success, doesn't it? She had a hard childhood, escaped privation, became rich and famous, and then ruined it all in a particularly public way. It's hard to watch somebody self-destruct that way."

I wondered if she thought I was guilty of the same self-destruction. Was she implying that I was ruining my life by not moving to New Orleans with Guidry?

I said, "Why would she do that?"

She shrugged, as if the answer were obvious. "She's older now, so she requires more drugs to get the same high."

Disappointed, I shook my head. "I don't think she does drugs."

"We all do drugs, Dixie. We're all drug addicts. Some of us are addicted to prescription drugs or street drugs, the rest of us are addicted to drugs we manufacture inside our own bodies. We like to believe our actions are based on logic or need, but in reality we're all ruled by our individual addictions."

My face must have shown that I didn't know what the heck she was talking about. She pulled her knees up and hugged them.

"Okay, a quick course in psychochemistry. Every emotion a person has creates a chemical in the brain that is instantly in every cell of the body. Each emotion creates a specific chemical. Opiates, depressants, sedatives, dopamine, we create them all."

She peered at me. "You're with me so far?"

"I think so, but —"

"No matter what it is, if we get a continuous supply of a chemical, our bodies will become addicted to it."

She stretched her legs out and waited a beat for me to catch up.

"Now imagine a child who grows up in a situation that causes her constant anxiety. Maybe there's not enough to eat, or maybe there's abuse. Whatever it is, constant anxiety means a constant supply of chemicals created by anxiety. The result is a child addicted to those chemicals. As she grows older, her circumstances may change, but the addiction to anxiety drugs will remain. To get the drugs, she will put herself into situations guaranteed to make her uneasy, or she'll interpret neutral events as threatening. However she does it, it's to ensure that her anxiety drugs continue."

I could imagine that child. I had known people who seemed to stir up unnecessary problems for themselves. Maybe I did it myself.

Reba said, "If that same child is praised for excelling at something, she'll also become addicted to the chemical that comes with the feeling of success. With those two addictions, she'll do everything she can to succeed in life so she can get more of the success drug, but no matter how successful she is, she'll create ways to feel anxious so she can get the anxiety drug."

Her eyes had taken on a new spark. It occurred to me that Reba was probably addicted to the chemicals she created while she was teaching.

She said, "Skydivers get addicted to the endorphins that come from free-falling, soldiers in combat get addicted to the chemicals created by episodes of intense danger, retirees feel lost without the old adrenaline rush of competition. It isn't the *behavior* that's addictive, it's the drugs created by the emotions that accompany the behavior."

I said, "That's kind of sad."

She laughed. "What's even sadder is that we can get the same hit of drugs by *imagining* the feelings that release them. People addicted to the drugs created by anger go around imagining angry confrontations. People addicted to drugs created by great sex spend a lot of time imagining sex. Or, conversely, if they're addicted to the drugs created by sexual guilt, they may go around thinking of shameful sexual experiences that are purely imaginary."

"So you think Briana —"

"Imagine what it would be like to be a poor kid breaking into houses to steal. Your heart would pound, your eyes and ears would be hyperalert. If you got into a tight spot you'd have to think fast to get out of it, and your only resources would be your wits and an agile body. You'd have to keep quiet about it, too, have a sly secret when you were with your family and friends. You would live with fear, excitement, triumph, relief, arrogance — emotions that would create a host of addictive chemicals."

I said, "So if Briana got addicted to those chemicals, she would have to find a way to keep her body supplied with them."

"Exactly. And in Briana's case, the way opened up like magic. She got noticed, she became a model, then a supermodel, and all the time she was lying about her background. The fear of exposure would give her the same old chemicals she got from breaking into houses. But over time, bodies require more of the old addictive drug to get the same satisfaction. So Briana would have had to do something to increase her fear of being caught."

"Like stalking Cupcake."

"That would be my guess. And since he was her companion when her addictions began, she might have got additional satisfaction just by being near him."

"But why wasn't Cupcake addicted to the same chemicals? He was breaking into houses with her."

Dryly, Reba said, "Have I missed something? Isn't he a famous football player? He has to move fast, be highly alert, be on top all the time, or he'll lose games and his career. That's excitement. That's anxiety. That's triumph. Those are emotions that create all the old chemicals he knew as a kid breaking into houses. He also got rewarded for doing a good job, so he would have dual addictions. Most people have a lot more than two."

As if she sensed that I bristled at the idea of Cupcake being an addict, she leaned over and patted my knee. "As I said, Dixie, we're all addicts. Every person in the world is addicted to several self-created chemicals. Our addictions can be productive and beneficial, or they can be destructive. In Briana's case, they seem to be self-destructive."

I thought about how Briana's and Cupcake's lives had diverged. Cupcake got recognition for his athletic skills. Briana shot the uncle who'd molested her for years. Cupcake had heard cheers and been offered scholarships. Briana had run away and became an anonymous face among other anonymous faces in the French Quarter of New Orleans. Cupcake had followed a trajectory that led to pro ball and an ability to express his innate generosity by helping underprivileged kids escape the same poverty he'd escaped. Briana had followed a trajectory that led to being a famous model, but instead of helping other young women dealing with abuse and poverty, she'd hung out with criminals. Perhaps Briana had only one addiction — to chemicals that came from flirting with the danger of public exposure.

Without meaning to, I blurted, "I think the investigators know who the murdered woman is, but they're saying they don't."

"You don't like people keeping secrets from you."

That's the problem with shrinks, they always bring it back to *you,* and what *you* feel. But she was right, I hate it when I know people are holding back something from me.

"I guess not."

"Well, that's the way law enforcement works, isn't it?"

I didn't even bother agreeing. We both knew why I hated secrets.

I said, "What do you think I'm addicted to?"

She smiled. "We all have to figure out our own addictions, Dixie, but I think one of your addictions is to chemicals that come from the satisfaction of seeing wrongs righted, justice done. You've been that way as long as I've known you. It's why you became a deputy, and it's why you'll always have an interest in criminal cases. Luckily for me and Big Bubba, you're also addicted to chemicals derived from the satisfaction of doing a good job as a pet sitter."

On hearing his name, Big Bubba yelled, "Whatcha doing there?"

Reba and I laughed, and I felt a ton of weight slide off my shoulders. At least I didn't have to carry around a false burden of trying to understand things that really didn't have anything to do with me.

12

When I got home, Michael's car was in the carport, but I didn't go inside the house to talk to him. I didn't trust myself not to blurt out all that had gone on. If I did, I'd create worries for Michael. I chuckled a little bit to myself when I thought what Reba would say about the way Michael worried about me and Paco. With our irresponsible mother, Michael had been protecting me all his life. The poor guy was probably addicted to the chemicals his brain cranked out every time he worried about somebody he loved.

I trudged up the stairs to my apartment, using the remote to raise the electric shutters over my French doors. The sun was directly overhead, but my porch's roof kept it from being blazing hot. A cardinal couple cooling their feathers on the porch railing watched me open the French doors and go inside. I lowered the shutters over the doors, plunging my apartment back into cavelike dimness. Except for the glass doors, the only light in my apartment comes from a small window over my kitchen sink and a narrow stretch of glass near the ceiling in my bedroom. An AC unit is wedged into an opening cut for it in my bedroom wall.

Shedding clothes like a cat shedding hair, I went straight to the bathroom and stood under a warm shower. Then I pulled on a terrycloth robe and fell into the rumpled bed I'd left that morning at four o'clock. My day had already lasted eight hours, and it had barely started.

I was asleep before I'd got my arms and legs arranged for it. I dreamed I was walking up a narrow mountain trail. On one side of me was a rough mountain wall with granite protrusions I had to duck to keep from hitting. On the other side was nothing, just space. I could see clouds below me, and what looked suspiciously like the moon. I turned a corner, and the trail came to an abrupt end. A red door with shiny gold hinges was set in the mountain face. The door had a golden doorknob. I reached for it, but the door flew open before I touched it, and a narrow red carpet unrolled before me. It marked a passageway to a tall throne at the far end of a cavernous room lit by millions of flickering birthday-cake candles set in little rosebud holders. The candles were pink.

On each side of the carpet were brown frogs in satin livery — white waistcoats and orange pants, and emerald green cummerbunds around their waists. They were frisky frogs, and as I walked forward they leaped and danced like Baryshnikov, clicking their heels together in midair and doffing white satin top hats while they sang in smooth harmony. I could not make out the words to the song because I didn't speak frog, and my ignorance of the language bothered me. As I got closer to the throne, I could see that a large black frog sat on it. I knew he was a king because he had a gold crown on his head and he was dressed all in white satin — tight pants, fitted vest, white satin cravat knotted at his neck, little white satin ballet slippers on his feet.

I walked to the very end of the carpet and looked up at the king.

He said, "What do you want?"

I said, "Well, sir —"

His bulgy eyes swelled and he yelled, "Do I look like a sir? Don't be calling me sir, I'm a king!"

So I said, "Forgive me, Your Majesty. I just want to know —"

He said, "You want to know! You want to

know! Always you want to know! You always want to know, don't you?"

I said, "Well, I just —"

"I know," he said, "you want to know the future. You want to know what's coming."

He leaned forward, and his eyes were like big yellow balloons about to pop.

"You know what, sister? You waste all your todays wanting to see tomorrow."

The other frogs leaped on me, and I shoved at them, struggling to get free.

I woke up kicking and grunting, with my robe twisted around my legs and one of the sleeve edges caught under my body so my arm couldn't move. My heart was pounding and I was breathing fast and my skin was still puckered from the clammy feel of frog bellies pressed on me.

I sat up and shuddered for a minute, then padded to the kitchen and made a cup of tea in the microwave. I stood at the sink and looked out the window while I drank it. That stupid frog king had made a point, and I'd got it.

Even so, I wondered why Ethan had chosen to meet me that morning. I wondered what he'd been about to ask me when Steven arrived. I felt as if I were on the verge of having to make a huge decision about my personal life, and I wasn't sure I was ready to make it. I had been a chaste widow for three years, and then I had been in a relationship with Guidry for a brief time. After Guidry moved to New Orleans, the relationship had been strictly via the phone. That wasn't a situation that could continue forever. The truth was that it was time to either completely sever the relationship with Guidry or change my mind and follow him to New Orleans. And as I had told Ethan, moving to New Orleans wasn't right for me.

I didn't want to think about it. I didn't want to face what had to be faced. People say that denial doesn't work, but it worked just fine for me. I could deny all over the place.

For the next couple of hours, I sat at the desk in my office-closet and took care of the clerical side of a pet-sitting business. When it was time to leave for my afternoon rounds, I got into clean cargo shorts, white tee, and fresh Keds, smoothed on sunscreen, put my hair in a ponytail, and grabbed my big carryall shoulder bag.

Out on my porch, I saw Michael down on his deck adjusting things on his prized outdoor cooker. Michael is big and broad and blond like a Viking warrior. He's also persnickety about his cooking equipment. Everything in his kitchen was built for professional chefs, and so is his barbecue stuff. Michael loves it all with a tender devotion. If he ever meets George Foreman, they'll probably spend a couple of days discussing the relative merits of charcoal and wood chips.

I clattered down the steps and went and stood beside him.

He said, "Grilled flank steak for dinner."

I said, "Um. With scalloped potatoes?"

"You bet."

Governments who send spies to gather secrets from other governments should send members of the same family. Nobody would be able to break their codes. In our brother-sister speak, Michael had just told me that Paco would not be home for dinner, because Paco doesn't eat meat and he doesn't like scalloped potatoes. Which meant that Paco would be at some undercover job that night, which neither Michael nor I would mention.

I told Michael I'd be home at the usual time and zipped off to see to my afternoon pet clients, beginning with Billy Elliot.

Tom and Billy Elliot were in the living room watching an old romantic movie on TV. I apologized for intruding, and they both hurried to assure me they were too macho to care about that girlie romantic stuff and that I was a welcome interruption. Billy Elliot did that by kissing my knees, and Tom by clicking off the movie with a very emphatic thumb, as if I'd caught him watching a porn flick.

Tom sported a lilac-hued knit shirt with a yellow polo pony embroidered on its chest. He had the shoulders-back posture of a man showing off a new purchase.

I said, "Nice shirt. Is that new?"

He beamed. "Guess what it cost!"

When somebody asks you to guess what they paid for an item, it's like somebody asking how old you think they are. You have to guess more than you really think they paid and less than you really think they look.

I said, "Twenty-five dollars!"

"Two fifty!"

I let my jaw drop. "No!"

"Found it at a consignment shop. They had a whole box of them, brand-new, still had the price tags on them."

"Ralph Lauren shirts for two fifty!"

He grinned. "Well, they had the Ralph Lauren polo pony on them, but the pony's tail was a little too bushy and the backside of the embroidery was snarled. And when I take it off tonight, I may have lavender-colored skin from the dye. But what the heck, it was only two fifty."

I held out my wrist. "My Rolex was only fifty dollars."

"I'm glad you didn't go for a diamond bezel. Plain is more tasteful."

"Yeah, and a diamond bezel would have been an extra five bucks."

He shook his head in mock sorrow. "All we have to believe in now is reality TV. Everything else is fake."

"You mean the reality shows where a guy's lost in the swamp, all alone, scared to death, thrashing around though the trees, while a director, a camera crew, a makeup crew, and a recording crew are filming him?"

Billy Elliot nudged me, and I bent to clip his leash to his collar.

Tom said, "They still haven't identified the murdered woman in the Trillin house. Wouldn't there be fingerprints they could check?"

I did not say, *They know who she is, they're just not saying!*

Instead, I said, "Not unless she's been arrested for a crime or fingerprinted for a job. Or if she served in the military."

"Maybe they know who she is and just aren't telling."

"Could be. They wait until they notify the family before they release a homicide victim's name."

"Still seems like a long time."

I stood up straight. "Tom, while Billy and I run, would you find out the exact time the Trillins' flight will arrive? They left from Parma, Italy, a little after midnight this morning, and I think they'll arrive in Sarasota around ten o'clock tonight."

Tom's round black eyes danced with curiosity, but he nodded without comment, and I led Billy Elliot out his front door.

Billy and I did our racer imitation on the track in the parking lot and went back upstairs. Tom was in the living room watching the same romantic movie he'd been watching when I first arrived. This time he only muted the sound when I came in. As soon as I took off his leash, Billy Elliot trotted to sit on the floor beside Tom's wheelchair and stare at the TV.

I hung Billy's leash in the foyer closet and grinned at them. "You guys watch the soaps, too?"

Tom said, "The plane you want is a US Airways flight from Rome to Charlotte, then Charlotte to Sarasota. It's expected to arrive here at nine fifty-five. That could change, but the weather is good, so it probably won't be off by much."

"Thanks, Tom. I appreciate it."

He flapped his hand at me and went back

to watching the movie. As I closed the door behind me, I heard movie music swelling to a tear-jerking ending. I was sorry I had ruined the movie for Tom and Billy but glad I had the exact information about the Trillins' flight. I wanted to talk to Cupcake before the law did. If nothing else, I could warn him that his secret about knowing Briana was going to be exposed.

My next stop was at a house where six cats lived. They were all rescues, and each of them had the grateful eyes that rescues always have. Their humans were two sisters who had a pact that if one wanted to bring another cat home, the other would stop her — by force if necessary. The sisters had gone to visit their ailing mother in Georgia, so for a few days the cats would have to make do with just me as a giver of goodies. With all the running and chasing they did, they gave one another plenty of exercise.

Leaving there, I realized I was on the same street where my grandmother's seamstress lived. I had taken a few things to Mrs. Langham myself — mostly pants or jeans to be shortened — and I knew she also designed and made women's clothes. On a sudden impulse, I swung into her driveway.

When I rang the doorbell, I heard her yell, "Come in!"

Hesitantly, I turned the knob and pushed the door open. "Mrs. Langham?"

"Come on in, I'm in the sewing room!"

I followed the sound of her voice and found her in a bedroom converted to sewing room, with a full-length mirror, a dressmaker's form on a stand, an ironing board set up with a steaming iron at the ready, and a pegboard with about a million spools of thread in every imaginable color on the wall. Mrs. Langham herself sat behind a sewing machine on which she was furiously sewing a narrow hem on a full skirt.

She had a tape measure hanging around her neck, and her pepper-and-salt hair looked as if she'd forgotten to comb it that morning. When she looked up and saw me, she laughed.

"Oh, Dixie! I thought you were somebody else."

"Mrs. Langham, you really shouldn't leave your door unlocked like that."

She laughed. "Been doing it all my life. I'm too old to change now. What can I do for you?"

"Nothing, really. I was just in the neighborhood and thought I'd stop in."

"Your mother used to do that. Of course, she always had something in mind she wanted me to make for her."

"You knew my mother?"

She looked exasperated. "I haven't always been this old, Dixie. She and I are about the same age, actually. Now *she* was a woman who knew how to dress."

She cast a dismissive look at my rumpled shorts and tee, as if to say that anybody in her right mind could see that I was *not* a woman who knew how to dress.

I said, "I remember. I was only nine when she left, but I remember how she dressed."

I didn't admit that I sometimes stole into the attic of Michael's house and lifted out musty-smelling clothes our mother had left in an old trunk. Her clothes were the only things she'd left behind for Michael and me.

Mrs. Langham said, "I made a lot of her clothes. She would see something in a magazine and bring me a picture, and I'd make it. We were both so young then, we had the nerve to tackle anything. Most of it turned out okay."

"You stole designs?"

She frowned. "I copied designs."

I reached out and twirled a spool of hot pink thread on its peg on the wallboard. "I guess I don't know the difference between stealing and copying."

Like a teacher explaining a simple idea to

a dull student, she said, "Here's how it works: A designer has an idea for a dress or a blouse or a skirt or something. It's not a better idea than you or I could come up with, but models show it in those big fashion shows where reporters and wealthy women in dark glasses go, and everybody goes nuts over the length of the skirts or the way the jackets have shoulder pads or the way they don't. Movie stars and wealthy women buy those clothes and pay thousands of dollars for a blouse or a pair of slacks. Counterfeiters rush out and copy the designs, put the designer's label in them, and sell a blouse or a pair of slacks for hundreds of dollars. Garment manufacturers copy the designs in different fabrics or colors and send them out to department stores, and a blouse or a pair of slacks will cost maybe fifty dollars. Dressmakers like me copy the designs in the same fabric and color as the original, and a pair of slacks or a blouse will set a woman back the cost of the fabric and whatever the dressmaker charged to make it. That's the difference."

"But counterfeiters can go to jail."

"Counterfeiters put a designer's label in their stuff. They claim it's the original goods. Dressmakers don't claim it's anything but a copy. That's the only difference."

"So it's the difference between an honest copy and a dishonest copy."

"Exactly. And if you ask me, the people who get stung by a counterfeit copy sort of ask for it. It's all about ego. They think having a big designer's label in their shirt makes them more important. You see people going around wearing scarves with designer's names on them, or carrying handbags with the designer's label on the outside. What's that about, for God's sake? If I'm going to put a name on something I wear, it'll be my own name."

She put her elbows on her sewing machine and leaned her chin on her folded hands. "Dixie, why don't you let me make you something nice to wear? You've got your mother's figure, but you hide it under all that droopy stuff."

I felt my whole body blush. "I'm a pet sitter. I have to wear this droopy stuff."

"I'm talking about when you go out. I'd like to see you in something wrapped in front, fitted close at the waist, with a deep cleavage. A dark rose color, I think."

My mind immediately went to shoes with ridiculously tall heels in which I stood beside Ethan at a nice restaurant where the tables were covered in starched white linen. Ethan's fingertips were on the small of my back. My dark rose, tightly wrapped back that was behind my deep-cleavaged front.

I said, "I don't go out much."

As if continuing a different conversation, she said, "How is your mother, anyway?"

While I was still registering the fact that it had been Ethan's fingertips on my back and not Guidry's, I said, "I haven't seen my mother since she came to my grandfather's funeral. She left right afterward, and we never heard from her again."

I didn't add that we'd never heard from her before Granddad's funeral, either, or that she'd left as soon as she'd learned that all my grandfather's assets, including the beachfront property, had been left solely to Michael and me.

"So you don't know where she is?"

"Not a clue."

"That's too bad."

I shrugged.

"Dixie, your mother wasn't a bad person. She just wanted more than the life she had here."

I thought of Briana saying, *I would have followed the devil himself to get out of that little town.*

I said, "She had two kids here."

"She knew your grandparents would take care of you. It wasn't like she put you out on the street."

And suddenly I was a child, walking down a long hallway where my mother's collection of hats covered an entire wall. The hats had hung on pegs the way some people display masks picked up in exotic locales. There hadn't been anything exotic about my mother's hats, and she'd bought most of them in Sarasota, but they formed a pleasing mosaic of colors and shapes on the wall. Every morning, Mom would come out of her bedroom still in her nightgown and walk back and forth in front of the wall of hats until she'd found the one that fit her mood for the day. Then she'd clap it on her head and disappear to dress in something that did justice to the hat she'd chosen.

When she left us, she didn't take her hats, so for a long time my brother and I had expected her to come home. We couldn't imagine how she'd manage to know how to feel without a hat on her head to direct her. It took me a long time to understand that she'd known all along how she felt. The hats had merely given her a daily role to play so nobody else would guess who she really was.

Mrs. Langham got up and came toward me with a tape measure in her hands. "Stand still, let me get your measurements."

She was a pro. Before I had time to tell

her I didn't really want her to make me a dress with plunging cleavage, she had measured me.

"I'll get the fabric and notions. Stop by next week and we'll do a fitting."

I wanted to tell her I had plenty of notions of my own, but I had a feeling she meant notions of a different kind.

I left her smiling to herself as if she knew some funny secret. As I drove away, I felt a sudden and totally unexpected stab of longing for my mother.

The rest of the afternoon went smoothly. No pet had peed on a rug or knocked over a potted plant. Every tail was raised in satisfaction when I left. After my last call, I went to the Trillin house to see how much progress the crime-scene cleaners had made.

I parked in the driveway behind their blue and white hazmat van. The front door was open, and I could hear the sound of a vacuum inside. I stuck my head in the front door and saw a man in a blue jumpsuit backing toward the door. He was pulling a vacuum hose that seemed to be sucking up moisture from the floor.

I waved my arms and yelled over the noise, and he turned his head to look over his shoulder. He wore a surgical mask. He turned off the machine and turned to face me, but he didn't remove his mask. With his hazmat gloves and boots, he looked like an extra on a movie about an invasion of aliens from outer space.

Through his mask, he said, "You can't come in here."

"I know. I just wanted to know what you'd had to do about the tile."

He hooked the mask with a finger and pulled it below his chin.

"Most of the fluids were in a rug, so the crime-scene techs must have got here fast and removed the body. The rug looks like an expensive Oriental, but I imagine it's a total loss. We didn't have to replace the tile."

"So when can the owners come home?"

"Cupcake Trillin lives here, doesn't he? I saw the photographs."

I smiled. "I just take care of the cats."

He nodded understanding. "They can come back tomorrow morning."

He pulled his mask up and turned his machine back on, and I hustled back to the Bronco and headed home.

The sun was already below the horizon when I drove down my shelled lane, the lane that curves to the place I've called home since I was nine years old. Except for the years I was away making a life as a deputy and a wife and a mother . . . But I try not to think about those years. The memory is too sweet.

I smelled smoke from the grill when I got out of the Bronco. The western sky was flushed with coral and pink light, and the air under the trees moved with a touch of coolness.

Michael opened his kitchen door and yelled, "Heat's almost ready!"

He meant that he had been sticking his hand over the grill to test its intensity and that he was beginning to be able to hold it still for a second or two without getting third degree burns. People who cook over open flames are masochists.

I hollered, "I'll be down in ten minutes!"

I really would be, too. I'm the world's fastest shower taker. Turn water on, get under it, squirt bath gel on a sponge, rub on body, stand a second, turn, stand another second, turn water off. That's it. And I can air-dry while I dash to the office-closet for clean clothes. No wasted time rubbing with a towel, no sirree. Just jump into clean cotton, shove my feet into flip-flops, run a brush through my hair and a tube of lip gloss over my mouth, and I'm ready. Not ready for Massachusetts or New York or Idaho, maybe, but ready for Florida.

Downstairs, Michael stood with a tray of marinated meat, gazing with adoration at his hot grill. Ella Fitzgerald sat on a chaise gazing at Michael with adoration. She wore her cotton harness attached to a leash attached to the leg of the chaise. Ella has an adventurous streak, and after Paco spent hours searching the woods for her, he decreed that she would henceforth be tethered when she was outside.

The deck table was set with thick pottery plates and black-handled flatware. Salad waited in a big wooden bowl for me to toss with vinaigrette Michael had made. A chilled bottle of wine was already open, ready for me to pour into two stemmed glasses. Along with going inside and getting the scalloped potatoes from the oven, those were my jobs. Michael's job was to stand by the grill and watch the meat so he could catch the exact moment when it was at the perfect stage of medium rare. It was our brother-sister routine perfected over many years.

Michael laid the meat on the oiled grill, and we both smiled at the sizzling sound it made. I knew Michael thought of our grandfather every time he heard that sound, same as I did. Our granddad had loved to grill as much as Michael does. He was the one who'd taught Michael to count the seconds he could hold his hand over the heat, and to slap the meat on when he could count to ten without yelping in pain.

I tossed the salad, poured wine, and scurried into the kitchen to get the pan of potatoes from the oven. Michael studied the meat, turned it once, pushed on it with a thumb to see how much it resisted. That's another test our grandfather taught him. When he thought it pushed back about like an athlete's thigh muscle would, he transferred it to a wooden board waiting by the grill and covered it loosely with foil.

He left it there and took his chair at the table. "We'll let it sit awhile before I slice it."

He always says that. For all his adult life, Michael has grilled flank steak and then said, "We'll let it sit awhile before I slice it." He says that because that's what our grandfather always said, and every time he says it and we wait for the steak's juices to settle in, we feel as if our grandfather is there with us. Maybe he is.

When Michael judged that enough time had passed, he went back to the grill and put Ella's portion on a plate and set it on the floor — cats shouldn't have anything with onion in it, so he hadn't marinated it.

She had already hopped to the deck floor with twitching whiskers, and attacked her chunk of beef with all the ferocity of a wild feline leaping on a small rodent in the woods. Cats love to pretend like that.

Michael picked up one of his knives that he keeps so sharp that I don't like to even get close to them. He sliced the steak very thin and on the diagonal because it's more tender that way. He piled several slices on our plates and moistened them with some of the marinade he'd heated on the grill. I added a scoop of scalloped potatoes from the casserole dish.

I had stopped thinking about Briana and the murder. I had stopped thinking about Guidry and Ethan. I had stopped thinking completely and simply let myself be.

Some moments are so perfect you wish you could freeze them forever. Right then, sitting under a pink-flushed sky and preparing to share a delicious meal with my big brother and Ella, was one of those moments.

13

While we ate, Michael filled me in on his last twenty-four-hour hitch. A fire had broken out in a mall restaurant kitchen during the night and threatened to spread to its neighbors. It had taken several hours to get it completely extinguished, then more time to get their equipment back on the truck. Then just as they got back to the station, another call had come in, for a residential fire. It had taken the rest of the night to get that put out and to make sure no sparks had drifted to the tinder-dry vegetation in a wooded area behind the house. Following that, there'd been a kitchen grease fire that had singed some cupboards before they got there.

Out of the blue, I said, "Michael, do you remember how Mom used to dress?"

His eyes narrowed. "I remember the times she was too drunk to *get* dressed."

"I mean her sense of style. She had great

taste, you have to give her that. Things like when to stop with the jewelry, or the handbag that matches the shoes. No matter how carelessly she might have seemed to choose what she wore, it was all carefully considered so nothing was done to excess and everything looked fresh and original. That takes an innate sense of style."

"You think that makes up for everything else?"

I took a deep breath. Michael has more bitter memories of our mother than I do because he bore the brunt of her alcoholic carelessness.

"I talked to a dressmaker today who knew Mom when she was young. She said Mom was just desperate to get away from here."

"Well, she got away."

I could tell Michael was in no mood to talk about our mother and how she had deserted us. To tell the truth, I was surprised that I was having softer feelings toward a woman who had walked out on us when we were already reeling from the loss of our father. Of course, she had been reeling, too, from the loss of a husband.

Unlike my fashionable mother's, my own wardrobe tended to consist of whatever was clean, comfortable, and available. I had always liked the idea that my mother would have wept if she'd known how little she had influenced me, but perhaps she had influenced me more than I realized. Who knows whether our choices are inspired by unconscious desires to emulate or to reject? I wanted to think that I was past adolescent rebellion, but it occurred to me that I might be as stuck in contrariness as my mother had been stuck in a backwater town with nobody to admire her taste in fashion except the snowy egrets and the steely-eyed herons.

I said, "Were you able to get any sleep after you came home?"

Michael's face relaxed. "Some, but I'm beat. I'm going to bed early."

I did an internal debate. I'm a grown woman, and I can come and go from my own apartment any time I please, thank you very much. But I'm also a member of a family, and if my car drives off at a time when I'm usually crawling in bed, I'll cause unnecessary worry.

I said, "I'm going to meet the Trillins at the airport later tonight. Their house won't be ready for them to sleep in until tomorrow, so I'm taking them to the Ritz."

He chewed for a moment, and I could tell he had some questions, but he was too tired to ask them.

He said, "Must be a bad feeling to know somebody got killed in your house."

That was all we said about it. After we finished eating and cleaning up, I kissed Michael and Ella good night and skipped upstairs with a clean conscience.

When I called Cupcake's cell phone I expected to leave a message, but he answered. He and Jancey were in the Charlotte airport waiting for their connection to Sarasota. He sounded stunned, as if he'd just been hit upside the head with a two-by-four.

He said, "We're watching the news about that woman in our house. I don't understand any of it."

I said, "We have to talk. I'm going to meet you in the terminal when you get off the plane. There will probably be a ton of reporters in the arrival area, so we'll skip baggage claim and leave by the front entrance."

"We checked all our bags."

"You can send somebody to get your luggage tomorrow."

"Okay." Shock and confusion had made him docile.

I told him I would give him and Jancey all the information I had when we were together, and ended the call. All I had to do now was get dressed in something more appropriate for traipsing through an airport and make the forty-five-minute drive to SRQ.

In case the bridge was up that connects the Key to the mainland, I left early. I wore white linen slacks and a fitted black knit top, espadrilles, and a coral beaded bracelet. I had on lipstick and looked like somebody who knew what the heck she was doing. I slung a slouchy bag over my shoulder, held the remote in one hand so I could lower the shutters as I went down the stairs, and stepped out on the porch.

I never saw what hit me.

Pain slashed clear through to my bones, a screaming, shattering assault that made me want to paint myself blue and take away all that red. Several figures brushed past me, and male voices muttered in a foreign language. Footsteps thudded, running room to room in my apartment. Something dropped on the floor and broke, and a voice was raised in a guttural sound that had to be a curse. I couldn't move, couldn't scream. I may have moaned, but I think not, because even taking a breath sent agony through my body. I don't know how long I lay on the porch floor. I think I drifted in and out of consciousness. The men left. I knew that. I sensed more than saw them file down the stairs and fade into the darkness under the trees lining the meandering lane from the street. I inched my hand along the porch searching for something, I'm not sure what. I suppose I had some innate instinct that told me to find a cell phone and press buttons even though I couldn't speak. Ages passed, and the pain drained away as suddenly as it had come, but it left a moldy taste in the back of my throat, a grated-cheese feeling like summer gone bad.

Gasping, I pulled myself to a sitting position and leaned against the porch wall. I ran my hands over my legs, felt each arm, ran my fingers through my hair looking for blood or a bump, shrugged my shoulders against the wall to find a sore spot. I found nothing. Even my ribs seemed unbruised. My attackers had been skilled at inflicting agonizing pain that leaves no physical trace. Like people whose profession is torture that can be denied. My guess was that they'd used a sap on me, along with an asp baton. A sap is a flat, leather, figure-eight-shaped weapon, its larger end filled with buckshot. You can hit a strong man on the back of the shoulder in just the right spot with a sap and he'll be out of commission and nauseated for several minutes. Hit him on the side of his thigh at the right nerve point with an asp baton and he'll be paralyzed for a while.

Gingerly, I pushed myself upright. I sidestepped to the door and looked into my apartment. It had been ransacked. Whoever had attacked me had expected to find something valuable there. I doubted that a group of men would attack me for the few items I own. An old TV, a microwave, and a clock-radio were slim pickings, but I had no idea what else they could have come for.

Michael's house was dark. The only sound was the chirping of tree frogs and the swish of surf on the beach.

While I groped for a decision about whether to wake Michael, call 911, or both, my purse made a trilling noise. I jumped like a spooked rabbit. It trilled again and I realized it was my cell phone. I knelt and pawed through my purse and grabbed the phone. The caller ID said TRILLIN.

My voice quavered when I answered.

Cupcake said, "We're waiting. Where are you?"

I said, "Somebody jumped me when I came out of my apartment. Several men, I think. Knocked me unconscious, mostly. They went through my apartment looking for something, then they left. I'm still on the porch. Still shaky. I'm sorry I wasn't there."

"My God, Dixie. Did you call the police?"

"Not yet." A thought hit me, and I felt even shakier. "Cupcake, this may have something to do with what happened at your house. Has anybody spotted you at the airport?"

"We left the US Airways terminal and we're sitting in the Delta terminal. It's empty and nobody's at the gate."

"You need to get out of there without being seen."

"I'll take care of it. What's your address?" He was beginning to sound more like himself, a sensible, take-charge kind of guy.

I gave him directions and went inside. I didn't close the shutters. I didn't expect the men to return.

My apartment was a mess.

In the bathroom, I stared at my reflection in the mirror. A woman with messy blond hair and wide astonished eyes stared back. I lathered my hands with germicidal soap for a long time, as if they had been contaminated by fear bacteria. I combed my hair. I brushed at spots of porch dust on my white linen pants. I felt as if I were tidying up after a dream that had been very disturbing but not real. Not the least bit real, because I had no bruises or scratches to show for it. Just messy hair and trembling hands.

I left the bathroom, got a broom and dustpan, and swept up a broken teapot in the kitchen. The kitchen wastebasket had been emptied on the floor, so I swept that trash up, too, and put it back in the basket along with shards of broken teapot. I went through every room picking up things that had been thrown on the floor. The desk drawer in my office-closet had been up-ended on the desktop, a jumble of paper clips, pens, packages of file cards and Post-its. My record book where I keep information about all my pet clients lay open and facedown with its pages ruffled as if some-body had thrown it in disgust.

The men who had attacked me had been pros at inflicting untraceable pain, but they'd been in such a desperate frenzy when they'd searched my place that they'd over-looked the only two places that might have yielded something valuable. It almost seemed as if they had taken their cue from movie sets with trashed apartment scenes — things tossed on the floor and the obliga-tory broken pottery, but nothing that couldn't be set right. They hadn't noticed that one of the tiles in my office-closet floor is removable. If they had, they would have found a safe where I keep a will and a few pieces of my grandmother's jewelry. They hadn't pulled my bed away from the wall, either. If they had, they would have found the hidden drawer built into its dark side where I keep the personal guns my husband and I used when we were deputies.

It was close to eleven o'clock when I heard the growl of a car engine downstairs. I went outside and leaned over the porch railing. The sky had darkened to dark purple, and a half-moon bathed the world in silver light. In its glow, I watched Cupcake and Jancey get out of a nondescript sedan. They moved heavily, as if the weight of gravity had pushed them closer to the earth.

I called, "Up here!"

Jancey led the way, both of them looking up at me with concerned faces. Jancey looked drawn and stiff. Cupcake's eyes were full of red road maps. The first time I met Cupcake, I'd thought he was the scariest-looking man I'd ever seen, but his habitual scowl was a protective shield to hide the sweetest, tenderest heart in the world. That tender heart was housed in a body roughly the size and color of an upended shiny black Volkswagen. A Volkswagen with the whitest teeth and the cutest smile I'd ever seen on anybody over the age of two.

I said, "Rough trip?"

Cupcake said, "A couple across the aisle had a baby that cried practically the entire way."

Jancey said, "Twenty-two hours is a long time to sit, even with layovers when we could stretch our legs."

Jancey was almost as tall as Cupcake, smart as a whip, and pretty the way Michelle Obama is pretty, with a natural elegance and warmth that can't be faked. She handled Cupcake the way a mother cat handles her kittens. Gently but firmly.

We did a kind of group hug there on my porch, with lots of shoulder patting.

I said, "What happened at the airport?"

Cupcake grinned, flashing the dimples that turned his face into a cherub's. "I just explained to a brother skycap that I needed to get out without cameras following me. He took us down some back hallways to an employee parking lot and gave me his car keys. I told him I'd get the car back to him tomorrow."

He sounded as if that was a perfectly reasonable thing for a skycap to have done. I guess if you're a famous athlete, you expect favors like that.

I motioned them inside. "The guys who hit me also broke my only teapot, but I can make individual mugs in the microwave."

Jancey said, "I'll help you."

Cupcake said, "I'd rather have a beer if you have one."

He sank his wide bulk onto the love seat and looked around my spartan apartment while Jancey and I made two mugs of tea and opened a bottle of Corona.

I said, "Did you eat on the plane?"

Jancey shook her head. "We planned to eat when we got home."

"Oh, Jancey, I'm sorry!"

I opened my minuscule freezer and peered in at a frost-encrusted box of enchiladas. She visibly shuddered.

I closed the freezer, got out some halfway decent cheeses from the refrigerator, and made a hurried plate of cheese and crackers and sliced apple. Michael would have been able to give them a satisfying meal. I gave them cheese and crackers.

In the living room, Cupcake made room for Jancey on the love seat. He ate a chunk of cheddar before he spoke.

"Okay, tell us what the heck is going on. Who was that woman who was killed in our house?"

I took a sip of weak tea for courage. We didn't have time to beat around the bush or spare anybody's feelings.

"I don't know who she is, but there's something else I have to tell you about Briana."

Wedged into the love seat, Cupcake and Jancey leaned forward slightly, intent on my every word.

Ignoring Jancey, I looked into Cupcake's eyes. "Briana told me that she knew you when you were kids. She said you lived in the same town and that you were close friends in high school."

Jancey stiffened, and her head whipped to stare at Cupcake.

He glowered at both of us. "The woman's a liar. A stalker and a liar."

I said, "She told me details about life in that town. Her family used to boil crawfish in a big pot. People sat in their yard and ate crawfish and drank beer. Did you know anybody whose family did that?"

"Everybody in Louisiana does that!"

"Maybe she used a different name then?"

"Dixie, I did not have a white girlfriend, not by any name."

"She said you weren't that kind of friend. More like close platonic friends."

He shook his head. "Not even that."

I took a deep breath. "She says you broke into houses together and stole things."

Jancey's head turned again. She looked

worried.

Cupcake looked less certain. "I never broke into any houses with a girl."

The sentence hung in the air for several moments.

Jancey said, "But she knows."

Cupcake's mouth tightened. "This is nuts."

His shoulders lowered. "Dixie, when I was a kid I did break into a few houses, but not with that model! It was just me and Robbie Brasseaux, a skinny white boy I knew from school. I didn't actually go in the houses, but that was mainly because I was too big and muscle-bound to crawl through windows. I mostly boosted Robbie up so he could get in, and then I stood watch outside until he came out. Robbie knew a guy we sold the stuff to. None of it was valuable."

I said, "What happened to Robbie? Did he maybe grow up to know international models?"

His smile was grim. "He didn't grow up at all. Nobody knows for sure, but he disappeared in the swamp, and people thought a gator probably got him."

Jancey and I shuddered.

I said, "Could he have told somebody about you two breaking into houses?"

Cupcake closed his eyes for a moment as

if he couldn't bear to look at my ignorance any longer.

"Robbie's folks were dead or in prison or run away. Gone, anyway. He lived with an aunt and uncle. Poor white trash, the uncle was drunk half the time. They had three boys about Robbie's age, all of them mean as wild boars. They bragged they took turns sodomizing Robbie. That was his life. He didn't talk to anybody. He was just a scared, hungry kid. He just did what he had to do to survive."

I didn't want to hear any more. It was too awful to imagine, and I'd heard enough to be convinced that Briana had heard the story of Cupcake's teen years from somebody. She had borrowed them and repeated them to me as her own past.

I said, "I don't know if Briana has told that story to anybody else. Maybe it won't go any farther, but I wanted you to be prepared in case she did."

"She's lying."

With a new note of fear in her voice, Jancey said, "I think Dixie means that if the media gets hold of that story, it won't make any difference that she's lying."

Cupcake looked from Jancey to me. The possibility didn't seem to have occurred to him that skycaps will guide you down secret hallways and give you the keys to their cars if you're a beloved athlete. But if you're a beloved athlete who falls from grace, you'll become the butt of jokes made by late-night comedians who never threw a ball, and the topic of sermons by pastors who never ran for a touchdown.

Cupcake said, "So what's going to happen to her?"

I said, "She'll be in custody until a hearing that will decide if she can be released on bail."

Trying to sound charitable, Jancey said, "The poor thing must be emotionally disturbed."

Cupcake and I hid our grins because Jancey's voice had an edge like a repressed Baptist saying, *I'm sure the rattlesnake that bit my foot had Christian intentions.*

I said, "Disturbed or not, she had no right to break into your home."

Jancey's charitable nature only went so far, so I didn't add, "Or wear your husband's shirt on her naked self."

I wondered if Jancey would think I was crazy, too, if she knew I'd got Briana an attorney.

I said, "Things will look better after we've had a good night's sleep."

Cupcake said, "I'm going to bed as soon

as we get home."

I said, "The crime-scene cleaners will have to finish their work before you can go home. I've booked you into the Ritz."

They turned red eyes on me like forest wolves.

Cupcake said, "What?"

Jancey said, "Crime-scene cleaners?"

I braced myself. They still didn't understand what had happened at their house. They hadn't allowed their minds to stretch around the facts and imagine the scene in its entirety. They hadn't seen a woman lying in a pool of her own blood. An adult human body contains about four or five pints of blood, depending on its size. That's a lot of blood to pour onto a floor.

As gently as possible, I said, "Blood has bacteria that seeps into cracks and crevices and gets into the air. It takes a specialized cleaning crew to sanitize a house where a brutal homicide has taken place."

They both flinched at the word "brutal," and Jancey's eyes filled with tears.

I hated to be the one to explain the ugly reality they'd come home to, but bacteria from a homicide victim's blood might turn out to be the least ugly thing I had to tell them.

I said, "You can go home tomorrow morning. I'll bring Elvis and Lucy home from Kitty Haven."

They had such worried faces that I searched for something to lighten the mood. "Elvis carried a slip of paper to Kitty Haven. It's still in his carry case. He'll be so glad to get it back!"

They tried to laugh, managed weak smiles, and trudged downstairs to their borrowed car to drive to the Ritz.

I closed the shutters and trudged to my own bed, but not to get into it. First I pulled it away from the wall and opened the secret drawer built into its dark side. The drawer was custom made, with carved niches for each of the guns it holds. After Todd died and I left the sheriff's department, both our department-issued guns had to be returned, but I still have our personal guns. I'm licensed to carry, and I qualify for all of the guns I own. I regularly practice with them, too.

My personal favorite is a snub-nosed .38 Special revolver with a rubber boot grip. I lifted it from its niche, loaded it with 125 g rounds, filled a couple of speed loaders for backup, and laid it on my bedside table. I did not intend to be caught defenseless again.

14

When my alarm went off at 4:00 A.M. next morning, I had slept three hours. My brain begged for more sleep, but my body crawled out of bed and dragged to the bathroom like a half-comatose slug. Still half asleep, I brushed my teeth, pulled my hair into a ponytail, and got dressed for the day.

Before I stepped onto the porch, I picked up my revolver from the bedside table and held it ready while the metal shutters rose to the top of the French doors and settled into their soffit. I switched on the overhead porch light and looked into every corner to make sure nobody was waiting for me to come out. Nobody was. My assailants from the night before were probably sound asleep, while I, the innocent one, was groggily creeping around with a gun in my hand.

I hit the light switch to plunge the porch back into shadows and closed the French doors. With one hand holding the gun, I started down the stairs, hitting the remote button with the other hand to close the shutters. Being on guard against attack or intruders takes forethought, common sense, and manual dexterity.

The salt air was cool and fresh. The trees glittered with fairy lights made by moonbeams bouncing off dewdrops. The vehicles in the carport shone with early-morning sweat, and seabirds sleeping on the cars assured me that nobody was huddled out of sight in the shadows.

In the Bronco, I slid the .38 under my thigh where I could quickly reach it in one move. Strictly speaking, that was an illegal place, because a Florida license to carry a concealed weapon stipulates that a gun has to be stashed in such a way that it requires two moves to get to it. Like opening a car pocket or a purse and pulling it out.

With my gun illegally ready under my thigh, I drove at a sedate pace down the lane to Midnight Pass Road, looked both ways, and made a careful legal left turn. At Tom Hale's condo building, security lamps made puddles of light on the parking lot's dark pavement. I parked in a well-lit visitor's spot by the front door, dropped my revolver in my pocket, and hustled into the bright lobby. Before I stepped into the elevator, I looked inside to make sure it was empty.

Billy Elliot met me at the door all smiles and wags and knee-kisses, and we trundled down the hall to the elevator. He must have sensed that I was operating with half-charged batteries, because he tempered his speed when we ran the parking-lot track. Greyhounds are considerate like that.

Upstairs, I whispered good-bye to him and left him whirling his tail and grinning.

The run had wakened my blood, so I drove off with more of my synapses firing.

Mostly, they were firing questions about the men who had attacked me. Who were they? What had they been looking for?

Coming so soon after the murder in Cupcake's house, I was almost certain the incidents were connected but couldn't imagine how. All morning long, while I felt the weight of the .38 in my pocket, my mind played with the question, but I never came up with an answer.

After I finished my last pet visit, I called Cupcake's cell phone.

Cupcake said, "We're waiting for room service to bring breakfast."

I suppressed a snide comment about people who didn't have to get up early and walk dogs and clean litter boxes.

He sounded edgy and achingly hollow, like

a man who hadn't eaten in over twenty-four hours. I hoped the Ritz's room-service people understood they had to bring large quantities of whatever they were bringing.

I said, "What about your luggage?"

"I called a friend, and he's driving the skycap's car to the airport. He'll get our stuff from baggage claim."

I heard Jancey's voice in the background telling him what to say to me.

He said, "Jancey refuses to wear the same clothes she wore all the way from Parma, so she can't get dressed until our luggage gets here."

"Have you talked to Sergeant Owens?"

"He said we could go home. The officer heading the investigation will come by later and get a statement from us."

Dully, I said, "I'm going to the Village Diner and have breakfast. Then I'll go get Elvis and Lucy and bring them home."

I figured we'd all feel better after a good breakfast.

When I parked in the diner's graveled lot, I took the revolver out of my pocket and locked it in the glove box. There are some places where it's just *wrong* to take a gun, even if it's legal. On the way to the diner's door, I passed a gaggle of men leaning over the opened hood of a sexy red Porsche. One of them, obviously the car's owner, was punching the air while he talked.

"It just spent a week at the dealer's! I just picked it up this morning!"

The other men looked sympathetic, all of them rushing to tell their own horror stories about their cars. They didn't even notice me walk by. Not that men always noticed me, but it was a bit deflating to know that a bunch of men were more interested in a car's innards than in me. Especially since I knew that not one of them knew what he was looking at when he looked inside the car.

Used to be that men prided themselves on knowing car engines. They'd gather in driveways with beers in hand and pop the hood — once they passed the age of fifteen they always called it "popping the hood" — and they'd all lean over and with their free hands diddle the hoses and wires and dipsticks. They'd pull out a spark plug and examine it like forensic scientists examining blood samples. Then they'd do whatever was needed to get the car engine running like a Swiss watch. Now, men open the hood and peer in and scratch their heads. They say, "Damned if I know what's wrong. You'll have to call a mechanic." Because it's all computers now, and not a man alive understands the car he drives. Women don't either, but then we never did.

I opened the diner door and stepped into its homey, steamy smell with a sense of gratitude. The diner's smells never change. It's something I can rely on.

Judy zipped out of the kitchen with both arms balancing plates of food. She stopped and looked solemnly at me.

She said, "It's a bacon day, isn't it?"

Until she said it, I hadn't known it, but I nodded in mute gratitude, like somebody who'd been crawling across an arid desert meeting a genie who asked if she'd like a drop of water.

I can't live without bacon. I try, God knows I try, and I can go weeks without giving in. Then one day I'll wake up and hear bacon calling my name. That's the day I go in the Village Diner with the whites of my eyes showing all around, and Judy signals Tanisha to start frying up a rasher of bacon for me. Tanisha knows how I like it — crisp enough to break if you look hard at it, with no disgusting curled fat ends or little swollen white pimples on it. Judy brings it on its own little special plate as befits something of importance, and I'm like that over eager dog on the commercial who loses his cool because he knows he's getting bacon-flavored kibble. Given a choice between sex with George Clooney or crisp bacon on toasted sourdough bread smeared with real mayo, a slice of ripe tomato, and a frill of lettuce, I'd take the BLT every time. Well, maybe not *every* time, but definitely some of the times. Once, maybe. Okay, never, but I'd imagine the bacon sandwich all the time I was making love to Clooney.

I waved to Tanisha on the way to the ladies' room to wash off the affection lavished on me by cats and dogs. Tanisha's broad face dimpled and she waved back. Next to my brother, Tanisha is the best cook in the world.

Passing the counter where people can watch TV while they eat, I saw Squatty Knox, a high school algebra teacher who has blighted the lives of Siesta Key students since my parents' time. Squatty earned his unflattering sobriquet because he was, well, squatty. Low to the ground, as Floridians say, which isn't the same as short. It's just squatty. When I was in his class listening to him drone on and on, I always tried not to blink because I knew if I blinked I'd never get my eyelids to come up again. I was also afraid I might fall into a coma and tumble out of my chair, which would have caught his attention and made him call on me to solve some algebra problem. I couldn't have solved an algebra problem if he'd set my feet on fire. I did the best I could to stare straight ahead without blinking, which made my eyeballs so dry that it's a wonder flies didn't settle on them.

Like everybody else at the diner counter, Squatty was staring at the TV the same way I once stared at him. He seemed mesmerized by footage of Briana in different designer clothes, at different fashion shows. An offscreen male voice identified each place, each designer, each season — "Paris, for Yves St. Laurent, the 2008 spring collection; Rome, the 2010 fall show, for Chanel; Vienna, for Versace . . ."

I walked on by, wondering at which show Briana had met a Serbian gangster who'd gone to prison for smuggling heroin in a shipment of fake Gucci watches. Aside from the fact that drug dealing and counterfeiting were crimes, they were crass acts, not the kind of thing a discriminating woman would admire.

I spruced up in the ladies' room, and when I left, Squatty was still engrossed in the TV screen, this time showing footage of Cupcake in action on the football field. All the other people perched on stools at the counter seemed equally fascinated. They seemed to be attached to the screen by invisible IV lines, getting infusions of painkillers by watching images of people whose lives seemed more interesting or more rewarding or more bizarre than their own.

At my regular booth, Judy had already put my coffee on the table. As I slid onto the bench seat, she appeared beside me with my regular breakfast along with the not-regular special plate of bacon. For a second there, inhaling the siren scent of fried hog fat, I drifted off to my own personal nirvana. Some people escape pain through watching TV, some through smelling bacon.

Judy said, "Everybody's talking about the killing at that football player's house."

She waited a moment to see if I'd take the bait, then raised an eyebrow a fraction when I got busy buttering my biscuit.

She said, "You're not talking, huh?"

"I don't know any more about it than you do."

"Except you were there when it happened."

"I was outside the house. I didn't see a thing."

She studied my face and got a worried look. "Well, that's good. Maybe now that the hunk is gone you won't be getting mixed up in murders anymore. I sure hope so."

I sipped coffee. She topped off the mug and waited. I salted and peppered my eggs. She sighed and went away. For some odd reason, I felt like crying. When an old friend pumps you for information and at the same time is concerned about you, it's a little bit like having a caring mother quiz you about the questionable kids you're hanging out with. Not that I ever had a mother who did that.

The bacon helped calm me. I nibbled its salty, crispy, tranquilizing, artery-clogging goodness and considered all the weird things that had happened, especially the weird thing that had turned me into a helpless victim of violence. It isn't in my nature to be a victim. I fight back, I stand up for myself, I don't let myself be used — but violent men had got away with disabling me while they ransacked my apartment. Instead of fighting back, I had lain there helpless as a dead snake, and I was still helpless because I didn't know who they were. Standing up for myself against those unknown men would be like fighting fog. If I hadn't had the bacon, I would have got really depressed.

I was so blissed out on bacon that I didn't

see Ethan until he was standing by my booth.

"Are you expecting another homicide investigator?"

I laughed. "No, not today."

He slid into the booth and waved to Judy, who trotted like a pony to bring him coffee.

She said, "Tanisha's scrambling your eggs. I'll bring them right out."

This time I knew he had planned his breakfast time to coincide with mine. It made me feel proud and scared at the same time. Ethan wasn't the kind of man to indulge in casual flings. If he went after a woman, he was serious about it. He also wasn't the kind of man to let a woman jerk him around. If I made a commitment to him, I'd damn well have to keep it or there'd be some high drama. Not that I didn't keep commitments, but I wasn't sure anymore how *long* I could promise anything to anybody.

He gestured toward the TV over the counter, where voices still gushed the same old words, and diners still hung off their stools absorbing every stale word as if it were new and fresh.

"The murder in the Trillin house seems to have taken over every minute of the news."

I shrugged. "A famous model broke into a

famous athlete's house, and then some mystery woman was killed in the house. If you were a reporter and you had a choice of talking about that or talking about a new downtown parking lot, which would you choose?"

He grinned. "I can't imagine myself a reporter."

"That's because you make things happen. Reporters tell about things somebody else has made happen."

"That's probably an oversimplification, but true."

"I know a psychologist who says we're all addicted to drugs our bodies manufacture in response to experiences we have. Even our thoughts create drugs we get addicted to."

"Psychoneuroimmunology."

"Excuse me?"

"That's what it's called. Means that chemicals infuse every cell in our bodies in response to our emotions, and those chemicals affect our health. Happy thoughts create healing chemicals, hateful thoughts create toxic chemicals."

Judy whirled to the booth and settled his plate in front of him. She poured more coffee in both our mugs, waggled her eyebrows at me, and whirled away.

It doesn't take a man long to eat scrambled eggs and dry toast. While he ate, I watched him and felt stupider by the moment.

I said, "Am I the only person who doesn't know about psycho-whatever?"

He laughed. "No, and you'll be glad to know that it was a woman who discovered there's no time lapse between emotions and the chemicals they produce. Dr. Candace Pert, very brilliant woman. She says our bodies are our subconscious minds."

I sighed. "You're too smart for me, Ethan. I'm a pet sitter. I only have two years of community college."

He ate the last bite of tomato and tossed his paper napkin into his plate. "Nobody in the world knows everything. You're ignorant about some things I know about. I'm ignorant about some things you know about. Being ignorant about particular things doesn't mean we're stupid. Stupid people can't learn anything new. You and I can learn if we're exposed to the things we're ignorant about."

"Do you want to go out with me?"

I hadn't expected to say that, it just came out.

Ethan reached across the table and touched my hand. "You know I do."

"I have to tell Guidry. I'd feel dishonest to see you and not tell him."

"I understand that."

I said, "I think all my cells are being flooded with nice chemicals right now."

He laughed and got to his feet. "Let me know when you're ready to move forward."

He left money on the table for Judy and left the diner. Judy came and stood beside me with curiosity radiating from her like heat from a stove, but she didn't ask any questions and I didn't volunteer any information.

I was too dazed by what had just happened to be able to talk. Without planning to, I had in one quick instant made a decision about my future with Guidry and acted on it. It was a decision I didn't like, a decision that I didn't want to make, but one that had to be made. In a way, I was grateful to Guidry for letting me be the one to make it.

I said, "I'll see you tomorrow," and slid out of the booth.

In the parking lot, ignorance of car repair had finally won out, and a cluster of men watched other men load the red Porsche onto a flatbed tow truck. The owner of the Porsche had the anguished face of a man watching his child go off to war. Nobody noticed me get in the Bronco, nobody saw me drive away. I was invisible in plain sight, the way Tom Hale had said Briana's criminal friend had been until he was arrested.

The Kitty Haven is just around the corner from the diner, so I was there in no time to get Elvis and Lucy. I carried their cardboard carriers inside and helped Marge settle Elvis into the one with his scrap of paper still in it and Lucy into the other. I paid Marge, put the receipt in my pocket to give Cupcake and Jancey, and lugged the carriers out to the Bronco. As if she realized she was going home, Lucy poked a paw through the air holes and made excited noises. Elvis was quiet. Probably sniffing his paper to make sure nobody else had played with it since he left it.

15

All the way to the Trillins' house, the phone call I would have to make to Guidry rode in the car with me like a little gray cloud. It was still with me when I pulled into the Trillins' driveway and got the cat carriers from the Bronco. Jancey saw me from the living room window and opened the front door before I rang.

She said, "Good timing! We just this minute got here."

She had an odd expression on her face — a normal reaction to returning to a house where a crime-scene cleanup team had removed all the familiar odors. Like other animals, humans rely on their sense of smell as well as their vision and hearing to recognize places and people. Take away the smell of your own home and it will seem alien.

In the living room, Cupcake was looking around like a tourist visiting a house of some historical figure.

I couldn't keep from looking toward the spot on the floor where the dead woman had lain. The cleanup guys had done an excellent job. Nobody would have guessed the floor had been awash with blood a few days before. If Jancey and Cupcake noticed the absence of a rug that had lain on the tile, they didn't mention it.

I set the cat carriers on the floor and knelt to open them. Each cat leaped out, Elvis carrying his beloved crumpled paper. Their ears flattened when they smelled the neutral air, and they both went hyper for a few minutes, racing around the room, leaping on furniture, generally acting like wild cats. Also a natural reaction to the absence of familiar odors in a familiar place.

After they had thrown enough of their own cells around to feel at home, they reverted to their sweet selves. Lucy rubbed her cheek against Jancey's leg to deposit scent cells on her, and Elvis trotted confidently toward the media room, still carrying his precious paper. Having marked her territory with cheek glands, Lucy made a chirping noise and galloped after her brother.

Cupcake said, "Dixie, Sergeant Owens said for us to go through the house when we got home and make a note of anything changed or missing. You'd better come with us. You'd know if anything was moved after we left."

I suspected they just wanted somebody else with them when they went through the house for the first time, but I would have felt the same way. We moved room to room, Cupcake and Jancey studying every piece of furniture, every picture, every curio. In the bathrooms, they stared at the towels and soaps as if they suspected them of being different than the ones they'd left there. In the kitchen, Jancey even pulled out drawers and looked inside them while Cupcake examined the interior of the refrigerator.

By the time we headed down the hall to the master bedroom, they seemed anxious in a different way. Personally, I was a wreck. I kept remembering the shirt Briana had worn the first time I saw her. I could imagine her tossing it on the bed and leaving it there for Jancey to find.

Jancey said, "If that bitch slept in our bed, I'm getting a new one tomorrow."

The shirt wasn't on the bed or on either of the two chairs in the room. The white silk duvet on the bed was smooth, too, and the artfully piled pillows showed no sign of having been dented by another woman's head.

But a pair of black sneakers sat in the middle of the duvet. The sneakers looked brand-new. Each shoe had the stark white Nike swoosh. Each was roughly the size of a loaf of bread.

For a moment, we all stared at the shoes without speaking.

Jancey said, "Cupcake?"

He said, "I didn't leave them there."

They looked at me, and I shook my head.

They strode to the bed and each picked up a shoe. They turned those Nikes over, examined their insides, pulled their tongues out, sniffed them, and then turned them over again and repeated each step.

Jancey said, "They're eighteen double-E's."

Cupcake nodded. "My size."

"Are you sure you didn't get them just before we left and put them here?"

"I didn't buy these shoes. I didn't leave them here."

They turned to me again, and I shook my head again.

I said, "I always make a fast pass through the house when I'm here just in case a cat has done something I need to clean up. Those shoes weren't here the last time I was in this room."

Cupcake said, "That would be the day

before that crazy woman broke in."

"Right."

Jancey said, "Cupcake, how does that Briana person know what size shoe you wear?"

"How the hell would I know, Jancey? I keep telling you, I don't know her!"

Jancey said, "You shouldn't wear those things. They could have radiation or flesh-eating bacteria on them that could kill you. Maybe you should give them to the police."

Cupcake looked like he might cry any minute, just from confusion.

In my head, over and over, I heard Briana telling about breaking into houses with Cupcake: *Cupcake mostly did it so he could get a pair of Nikes.*

Jancey pulled back the duvet to uncover pale pink sheets neatly tucked under the mattress. Her face relaxed. "I don't think she got in our bed."

Cupcake said, "Jancey, I swear to God I never knew that woman. I've never talked to her. I don't know anybody else who knows her."

I said, "Maybe it wasn't Briana who left the shoes. Maybe it was the woman who was murdered." I didn't believe that, but I wanted to.

Cupcake closed his eyes. "God, I'd forgotten about her."

Shamed, Jancey said, "Me, too."

Cupcake said, "Dixie, don't you think it's peculiar that nobody knows who that woman was?"

I said, "She didn't have any identification on her body. No wallet, no purse, nothing with a name or address on it."

"Couldn't they tell from fingerprints?"

I told him the same thing I'd told Tom Hale. "Some people live their entire lives without being fingerprinted. There's also a DNA database, but DNA is only collected in criminal cases."

Jancey said, "You'd think her family would report her missing."

"Maybe there is no family. Maybe she's a loner that nobody misses."

For a moment, my mind snagged on all the things we didn't know — gaps in personal histories, holes in life stories, dark secrets that could cost another life. Briana was either from Switzerland or Louisiana. She had or had not known Cupcake as a kid. Somebody had left a new pair of Nikes in the middle of the Trillins' bed, and nobody knew why. Men who spoke a foreign language had hurt me very badly, but I had no bruises to prove it. A woman had been murdered and nobody knew who she was.

In the media's coverage, the murder in Cupcake's house had been merely an excuse to explore Briana's glamorous life and Cupcake's sports history and philanthropic activities. When the dead woman was discussed at all, it was merely to give the particulars of her color, size, and approximate age. There hadn't even been the usual nattering talk shows about how odd it was that not one but two women had broken into Cupcake's house that morning.

The doorbell rang, and we snapped to attention.

I said, "I'd better go home now. Call me if there's anything I can do to help."

We all moved toward the front door, and Cupcake opened it. The homicide detective, Steven, stood outside.

He said, "Mr. Trillin? I'm Steven Jorgensen, with the FBI."

Catching sight of me, he looked embarrassed.

When Cupcake introduced me and Jancey, Steven said, "Ms. Hemingway and I have met."

I said, "Except you told me you were a homicide detective with the sheriff's department."

"You *assumed* I was a homicide detective."

He had me there. When I thought back to our conversation at the diner, I had to admit he'd never actually said he was with the sheriff's department. I had, as he said, *assumed* he was because Sergeant Owens had told me "the investigator" would be stopping by the diner to talk to me. I planned to have a little talk with Owens about that, but I should have known the FBI would get involved in the case. They always come in when state lines have been crossed in a crime. In this case, international lines had been crossed.

Cupcake gave us a puzzled frown.

I said, "Steven talked to me about the murder. I didn't realize he was with the FBI."

Steven said, "Actually, I'm just on loan to the FBI. I'm with Interpol."

Cupcake said, *"Interpol?"*

He sounded as if Interpol was just one damn thing too much. His glower was enough to cause the most hardened criminal investigator to quake.

It caused Steven to look defensive. "Interpol is an intelligence and liaison agency. We get involved in cases where law enforcement agencies of different countries have to cooperate." Turning to me, he said, "Actually, I'm glad to have a chance to talk to you and

Mr. Trillin together."

I knew what that meant. If he questioned us together, we wouldn't be able to give each other a heads-up if we told a lie.

Jancey said, "We can talk in the kitchen. I'll make coffee."

He said, "That would be nice, Mrs. Trillin."

Jancey led the way and we all traipsed to the kitchen, where everything was warm wood and cold stainless steel, with a swan's-neck faucet at the sink tall enough for a child to stand under and take a shower. Cupcake and Steven waited until I sat down at a round oak table; then they took chairs while Jancey bustled around filling a coffeepot and attaching it to a machine that looked as if it had come off a space ship. While the coffee machine sighed and gurgled, she got down black glazed coffee mugs, asked if anybody took sugar or cream, got a united no, and went to the freezer, where she took out a plastic bag of cookies and shook some on a black pottery plate.

She put the plate on the table, and we all leaned toward the scent of chocolate chips. It may have been my imagination, but Steven's eyes seemed to go a shade lighter.

He said, "You freeze them?"

She nodded. "As soon as they're cool from

the oven. Makes the chocolate set up, and they're crispier after they're frozen."

She moved gracefully to pour coffee, and Steven watched her. When he looked back at Cupcake, he had a new respect in his eyes. Everybody fawned over Cupcake because he was a great athlete. His close friends knew he was also a great guy, but his adoring fans only knew that he was a powerhouse on the football field. That's all Steven had known, too, but now he was seeing another side of Cupcake. The side that had a beautiful, gracious wife who baked chocolate chip cookies with extra care and served them with dignity and charm. A man with a wife like that is more than a big athlete, he's a man who has earned the love of a discriminating woman. Seeing that Steven recognized that and respected it made me look at *him* with a bit more respect.

I was becoming so comfortable with the man that I was almost on the verge of asking him where he was from originally. As if we really *were* just folks having coffee and cookies together.

Jancey wasn't as easily seduced as I was. Pointedly looking from me to Cupcake, she said, "Tell him about the shoes."

Cupcake said, "That woman left a pair of

Nikes on our bed."

Steven's eyes lit. "Could I see them please?"

Jancey said, "I'll get them."

We waited silently until Jancey hurried back with the shoes.

Just so I wouldn't look like I never had an original idea, I said, "It could have been the dead woman who left them."

Steven grunted and examined the shoes the same way Cupcake and Jancey had done.

He said, "Nikes mean anything to you, Mr. Trillin?"

Cupcake chuckled. "Only that I grew up poor, and wearing a pair of Nikes meant you were *somebody.* You walked tall if you had Nikes."

Steven pulled a penknife from his pocket, sank the tip inside one of the shoes, and popped out the insole. I wondered why I hadn't thought to do that.

He said, "Poor kids still covet Nikes. If you ask a ghetto kid why he started dealing drugs, nine times out of ten he'll tell you it was so he could buy a pair of Nikes."

Steven set the shoes side by side with their heels toward us. "See how the top edges aren't symmetrical?"

Now that he mentioned it, I could see that

one shoe's top edge slanted slightly to the left.

Like a magician playing his audience, Steven turned the shoes so their swoosh logos were facing us. "An authentic swoosh is curvy. These are angular. Now look at the stitching. See how some stitches are longer than others? And see how the material is rough at the edges? Look at the laces. Notice the broken fibers that give them a slightly fuzzy look."

He held a shoe to his nose and inhaled. "A heavy glue smell is always the first give-away."

I said, "They're fakes?"

He nodded. "Not even good fakes."

In an aggrieved voice, Cupcake said, "That woman brought me fake Nikes?"

He sounded so offended that Jancey and I started to laugh, but then we remembered the woman who'd left them had been either a murderer or a victim of murder.

Steven said, "Counterfeit sneakers make up about forty percent of the goods smuggled into the United States every year. The majority of those goods are fake Nikes. Some of them are obvious fakes. Some are so good even Nike's people would have a hard time telling them apart from the authentic ones."

I wiggled my toes in my Keds. "If they're that good, does it make any difference?"

Steven's eyes grew frostier. "It matters to the company with legal rights to manufacture and distribute them. It matters to the people whose jobs go to Asian sweatshops. It matters to the counterfeiters who make billions but pay their workers only pennies a day."

Cupcake said, "It matters to me! If I pay for real Nikes, I don't want fakes."

Steven said, "So does every other consumer. But the prices for fake goods are enticing: A handbag exactly like the original that sells for fifteen hundred dollars may sell for six hundred, and the buyer will think she got a bargain. The only items almost impossible to fake are things like a six-thousand-dollar Cabat handbag. Women who know that bag are savvy enough to recognize when the leather weaving is inferior."

I swallowed wrong and had a coughing fit at the idea of somebody spending six thousand dollars for a handbag. Any woman who would do that should just go whole hog and spend ten thousand for a new brain.

When I'd got myself under control, Steven said, "Other high-end labels are particularly easy to copy. Two-thirds of expensive timepieces are actually fakes."

I turned my wrist so the fake Rolex was facedown. I'd never pretended it was a real Rolex, but it was still a rip-off of the genuine article.

I said, "I don't understand how they get away with it. Isn't that what customs inspectors are for?"

"They catch bad fakes, but it's impossible to spot good fakes with a cursory inspection. Fakes don't come all in one shipment, either, or with one point of origin. A single shipment may contain fake Pradas, Fendis, Guccis, Versaces, all the top brands, all with falsified labels of origin."

Jancey said, "I've always known there were fakes, but I never realized it was such a big problem."

"Most people don't, but high-fashion counterfeiting rings have tentacles all over the world. The goods are distributed to upscale shops in resort areas such as the one you live in."

Jancey and I looked at each other, and I could tell she was thinking the same thing I was: *Which* shops, and had we ever bought something there? Since my fashion choices are more likely to come from Target or JC Penney's than a haute couture shop, I didn't imagine I had bought any good fakes. Jancey shopped at those high-end shops, though, and she might very well have bought a fake and not known it.

Steven said, "Versace just won a twenty-two-million-dollar settlement in a Los Angeles counterfeiting lawsuit. We found seventy-two retail stores in California and Arizona passing off fake Versace merchandise and charging for the real thing."

Jancey said, "Those stores *knew* the merchandise was fake?"

Steven smiled grimly. "Nobody sells counterfeit merchandise by mistake. If you sell a genuine Gucci watch, your profit margin is slim. If you sell a good counterfeit Gucci watch, your profit is large. For a lot of retailers, it isn't a difficult decision to make."

Jancey said, "What does all that have to do with a woman breaking into our house and killing somebody?"

Steven said, "That's the big question, Mrs. Trillin. I was hoping Mr. Trillin might be able to shed some light on that."

Like a scudding cloud, Cupcake's face went from confusion to recognition to anger in about two seconds. "You think I have something to do with fake Nikes?"

"If you do, or if you know anybody who does, now would be the time to say so."

Like a mother lion whose cub has been

threatened, Jancey stood up. For a moment it looked like she might snatch the plate of cookies off the table.

"Don't you dare imply that we're criminals! We were in Italy on the first vacation we've had together in years. We got a call from Dixie saying a crazy woman had broken into our house. We cut our trip short and made reservations to come home, but then we got another call saying the woman was murdered before the cops could come and throw her out of our house. Except it wasn't that woman, it was some other woman, and the first woman, the crazy model with one name, disappeared. Then we got to the Sarasota airport after twenty-two hours of worried travel, but Dixie couldn't come get us because she was lying on her front porch knocked out by some thugs who ransacked her apartment. Now, to add icing to our cake, you waltz in here and hint that Cupcake is making fake sneakers! Talk about adding insult to injury!"

Steven's eyes cut to me, and this time they weren't flat. "What thugs?"

I said, "It happened last night. About nine o'clock. I stepped out my front door and somebody slammed me so hard I almost lost consciousness. Probably used a sap and an asp baton. I lay on the porch floor and drifted in and out of awareness while some men trashed my apartment. I don't know what they were looking for. They left, and I got up and called Cupcake."

"Did you report it?"

"I didn't want to worry my brother. He was next door asleep, and he's a little bit overprotective, so I didn't want him to know. Besides, I didn't have any evidence that it had happened. No bruises, no bumps. No broken bones. No scratches. My ribs weren't even bruised."

"But the pain was so great that you fell down semiconscious."

I sank lower in my chair remembering it. "They were pros."

"When those men were in your apartment, did you hear any conversation?"

"They spoke a foreign language I didn't recognize."

"Did they take anything?"

"I don't think so. They threw things around, broke a teapot."

"For effect? Or in a real search?"

"I don't think they searched thoroughly. I don't know if they left everything a mess to make it look like they had searched or if they were just incompetent."

"Yet you thought they were professionals when it came to knowing how to incapacitate you without leaving evidence."

"You think they weren't really looking for anything? That they just wanted to hurt me?"

"I don't know what their intent was, Ms. Hemingway, but if you meet them again, please report it. Even if it causes your brother worry."

"Do you know who they could have been?"

"I have no idea."

His eyes had gone flat and bleak again. I wondered if that was something he did on purpose to hide when he was lying.

Steven sat up straighter. "I want you all to listen very carefully. I'm not at liberty to give you particulars, but certain transnational criminals seem to believe that you are a threat to their business."

With a nod toward Cupcake, he said, "Each of you has been thoroughly investigated. We have not found evidence linking you to any crime, but somebody believes you are, and you must be extremely careful until this investigation is resolved."

In one voice, Cupcake, Jancey, and I said, "You *investigated* us?"

He met our angry glares with a shrug. "Don't take it personally. Remember that

FBI stands for the Federal Bureau of *Investigation.*"

Jancey blew air like a horse snorting. "Don't take it *personally!* How else can we take it?"

"Mrs. Trillin, get your priorities straight. You aren't in danger because the FBI has investigated you. You're in danger because a criminal organization believes you have information or property they want."

Again in unison, we all said, "*What* information? *What* property?"

He looked from face to face as if he couldn't believe he was in the company of such idiots. Personally, I was studying him with the same cautious scrutiny I'd give a strange dog whose tail wagged while his neck hairs bristled.

16

Steven took the Nikes with him when he left.

Cupcake and Jancey were confused and angry.

I was confused and afraid.

We wasted several minutes asking one another what in the world international criminals could believe we had that they wanted. Then we wasted more minutes asking one another who the people could be. We knew they had to have something to do with selling fake merchandise. We knew the fake merchandise was most likely designer clothing or jewelry. And we knew that Briana had something to do with selling it.

I told them about the article Tom had found that linked Briana with a Serbian gangster who'd been sent to prison for shipping heroin in a crate of Gucci watches. They thought that was mildly interesting but couldn't imagine what it had to do with them.

Then I gutted up and said what I'd been thinking ever since I saw those Nikes in the middle of the Trillins' bed.

"Cupcake, when Briana told me that she robbed houses with you when you were kids, she said you mostly did it so you could buy a pair of Nikes."

Jancey glared at him. "You do know her, don't you?"

Cupcake stood up like a whale breaching. "I do not know a woman named Briana! I have never known a woman named Briana. The only kid I ever broke into a house with was a guy named Robbie Brasseaux. I never broke into any house with any girl."

He was so obviously sincere that Jancey and I went silent and ashamed, like kids caught stealing money from a church collection plate.

Cupcake made a sudden involuntary movement, a tic so small that Jancey didn't notice. I glanced at him as a spasm of pure despair floated down his face.

Under his breath, he whispered, "Sweet Jesus."

At the same moment, Lucy trotted into the kitchen, and Jancey turned her head to watch Lucy hunker over her water bowl and lap water with her sticky little tongue. Lucy wiped her face with her paw as if it were a napkin and trotted out of the room.

Cupcake said, "I have to get some sleep."

Watching him leave, Jancey said, "The only thing that makes sense is that Robbie Whoever told another kid about robbing houses with Cupcake, and the kid he told must have grown up and somehow met Briana and told her that he came from the same town as a famous athlete named Cupcake Trillin. Just gossiping, you know, making himself important by telling that Cupcake was a thief when he was a kid."

It seemed like an improbable coincidence.

"But why would Briana break into your house and leave fake Nikes?"

"A sick joke, maybe."

"Maybe, but it's not very funny."

When we'd said every useless thing we could think of twice, I left her and headed home. I knew I had to call Guidry before much more time passed, and the thought made me want to pull to the side of the street and cry. Besides, I was so tired my eyelids were sticky. All I wanted to do was have a nice warm shower and crawl into bed for a long nap.

Then, at the intersection leading to Oleander Acres, a surge of anger brought fresh memories of being laid out on my porch like a poleaxed heifer, helpless, frightened, and humiliated. I still didn't know what my attackers had hoped to find in my apartment, but I knew it had something to do with Briana and fake Nikes.

Energized by indignation, I turned the Bronco into Oleander Acres.

This time, instead of stopping across the street from the house where the man driving Briana's Jaguar had gone in, I pulled into the driveway. The man who answered the door was Asian, about forty, with a thin mustache and a wiry body balanced on the balls of his feet. We looked at each other for a moment, he with the inquiring eyes of somebody answering a door to a stranger, me trying to see any sign of recognition on his face.

I said, "My name is Dixie Hemingway. I'd like to talk to you about Briana Weiland."

His face altered, a perceptible tightening of muscles that gave him a fierce look. "Are you police?"

"No."

"Then I have nothing to say to you."

He backed away to close the door, and I stuck my foot in the doorway. "Please. It's very important."

"Important to your newspaper, yes. To

me, no."

"I'm not a reporter. Last night somebody attacked me and ransacked my apartment. I think they were connected somehow to Briana. I have a right to know who they were and why they came to my apartment. I saw you driving Briana's car, so I know you are close to her."

Behind him, a woman's querulous voice said, "What is it? Who are you talking to?"

He turned his head. "A lady asking about Briana."

The woman spoke rapidly in a language I didn't recognize, all vowels with varied inflections. I wondered why the neighbor had thought it was French.

I said, "Please, may I come inside?"

He stepped back. "Enter."

The house was typical Floridian upper-scale rental — pale tile floors, neutral walls, furniture with pastel linen cushions on bamboo frames, glass-topped tables. The woman was not the typical tourist. She was too thin, too intense, too angry. Asian like the man, she had short spiky black hair and the creped skin of a heavy smoker. She glared at me with black eyes that glittered like a trapped raccoon's.

In heavily accented English, she said, "Why do you let her in? Why?"

He said, "Please, Lena."

"No! No *please Lena!* I am done with it all. She has brought us to this. It is done!"

The man spoke sharply in their language, with a warning, cautionary note in his voice.

I said, "Were you one of the men who attacked me last night?"

All the belligerence seemed to drain from the woman.

She said, "Men attacked you?"

"Yes. They were waiting outside my front door. They hurt me badly, but they didn't break any bones or leave any scars. They had to have experience in inflicting great pain without leaving evidence."

The man said, "What language?"

"I don't know." I hesitated, then spoke what I was thinking. "It was not the language you two just spoke."

The man sighed and gestured toward a sofa. "Please to sit."

They took chairs, and for a moment we all assessed one another. I was searching for signs of duplicity or trickery, and I suppose they were doing the same.

The man said, "Those men who attacked you, they were experts at inflicting pain without breaking bones or leaving bruises, yes?"

"Yes."

"Then it is possible that you were attacked by members of a Serbian security company. If so, there will be no record of their presence in this country, and you will never find them."

I felt a buzzing in my head, as if bees were circling me. The man spoke as if it were a perfectly reasonable assumption that men with a Serbian security company would attack me on my porch, ransack my apartment, and then run away.

I said, "That's ridiculous. I have no connection to Serbia."

Lena laughed. "Ah, but you are a friend of Briana's."

The buzzing in my head grew louder, and I felt a hysterical urge to laugh with her. The entire conversation was insane.

I said, "Can we start over? I'll give you my name, and you tell me yours, and then we can have a rational conversation."

The man smiled, and I sensed that he pitied me.

He said, "Very well. You have already given us your name of Dixie Hemingway. You may call me Peter, and my wife is Lena. We are employees of Briana's. I drive for her, arrange for her travel, accompany her as a guard when she is in a crowded place. My wife is housekeeper and cook."

Lena said, "No more. I don't do that anymore. I'm done with it all."

I said, "I take it that you don't like Briana very much."

With a contemptuous glare, she said, "You are a fool, like all Americans."

Peter said, "Lena, you go too far!" To me, he said, "You must forgive my wife, please."

I leaned forward and spoke very slowly, as if I were speaking for an official record that would be buried in a time capsule.

"I'm a pet sitter. I go to people's houses and feed their dogs and cats. I have no involvement with Briana. I never heard of her until yesterday. I have nothing to do with Serbians or counterfeit shoes."

Peter and Lena exchanged a look.

Peter said, "Why do you mention shoes?"

"Briana left a pair of fake Nikes in the house she broke into."

Lena threw up her hands. "You see? She is a great fool! That is why I am done with her!"

Peter said, "Lena!"

Turning to me, she said, "You are soft and stupid! You know nothing of the real world! You grow up with food, clothing, everything! It makes you stupid. When I was a child I lived at the base of a mountain so tall it blotted out the moon. Soldiers came and killed my parents. I could hear them screaming and I could see the lights from the guns but I could not see the soldiers' faces and they could not see me. When the day broke I wrapped my feet in rags and tied some bread into a scarf of my mother's and started walking. I did not know where to go, I just walked. You ask about shoes. You, who have always walked in shoes, have always had unbruised feet. You have no idea what it means to bleeding feet to have shoes! And nobody, no government, no police can say it is wrong to give shoes to poor people to wear."

Peter said, "We know nothing about any shoes."

Lena said, "Ha!"

"Does Briana have something to do with counterfeit shoes?"

Before Lena could speak, Peter said, "The only thing I can tell you is that Briana is attracted to men of power, and she does not care how they use it."

"So Briana is involved with somebody who has something to do with counterfeit shoes?"

"Shoes, watches, shirts, wedding gowns, sweaters, handbags, heroin, many things."

"A Serbian gangster who shipped heroin in a crate of counterfeit Gucci watches?"

Lena's dark eyes had begun to watch me the way a cat watches a lizard trapped between its paws, as if the prospect of my ultimate decapitation was highly interesting.

Peter said, "You might say that."

Tom had said Briana's Serbian gangster had been murdered in prison — but gangsters are called gangsters because they have gangs, and gangs have secondary leaders who assume control after the first leader dies.

I said, "You're saying that this unknown Serbian person's spies saw me with Briana, so his security people put me out of commission while they went through my apartment looking for something."

Lena said, "Did they find it?"

I said, "Find what? I don't know what they were looking for! Do you?"

Her shoulders drooped, and she shook her head.

I had reached the limit of my ability to intuit or interpret or understand their clues. I had also reached the limit of my patience.

I said, "Okay, let's say you're right about all that. But who was that woman who was killed in my friend's house? And what was she doing there?"

Lena's lips pinched into a tight line. Peter's face closed. His eyes became opaque. "We know nothing about that."

Several moments passed. Nobody spoke, not even Lena. I believed they knew a lot more than they were willing to tell me, but I wouldn't get any more from them.

I stood up. "Thank you for talking to me."

Peter said, "Do you know now what you must do?"

It seemed an odd question, but English was not Peter's first language, and I thought he had simply worded it awkwardly.

I said, "It isn't my job to solve a crime or apprehend a criminal, but I understand Briana a little better now, and I suppose I'm a little closer to understanding what happened to me last night."

He walked me to the door. As I left, Lena spoke quietly behind me.

"May God protect you."

17

I drove home in a daze. From the moment I'd stepped into the Trillins' house and found Briana there, everything had been wrong side up, confused, and confusing. The only thing I knew for sure was that I didn't know anything for sure. Nobody was who they appeared to be. Everybody was dragging around some old shucked-off identity like snakes pulling shed skins that wouldn't let go. It seemed like life was falling into sync with technological fraud. I felt like a leaf caught in a rushing river, swirled by forces I hadn't even known existed.

When I was growing up, the landscape of my imagination was bounded on the south by exotic Miami, on the north by business-like Tampa, and on the east by Orlando's theme parks. All the other places on the globe came to me as televised footage of native villages flattened by storms or wars or floods. They were as disconnected from me as the craters on the moon.

That was no longer true, not for me and not for anybody else in Florida. On any day, one could hear Bulgarian shoppers at Publix discussing the merits of the tomatoes, Laotians inquiring the age of the fish, or Czech or German or Italian or French or Peruvian shoppers disparaging American yogurt. I liked the idea that we attracted all those bright, world-traveled sophisticates. Unfortunately, we also attracted some of the world's worst criminals.

Now it looked as if some of them believed I was a personal threat.

Michael's car was gone from the carport, which meant he was either fishing or buying groceries. Michael buys vegetables and fruit the way women buy shoes. He figures you never can have too many.

Before I got out of the Bronco, I took my .38 out of my pocket. I held it close to my side as I went up the stairs, pressing the remote to raise the shutters with my other hand. The air was hot and leaden. Branches on the trees hung heavily, as if they had absorbed so much moisture from the air they couldn't hold their heads up. The sun had moved to one o'clock, glazing the edge of the porch with bright light that reflected on the French doors.

Feeling as heavy as the trees, I held the gun ready until I was inside and the shutters had rolled to the floor. Ella wasn't in my apartment, which told me that Michael would not be gone long. After all that had happened to make me feel especially vulnerable, I liked knowing that he would be home soon.

I tossed my shoulder bag on the living room love seat, lay the gun on my bedside table, and took a shower. Water sluiced away the day's accumulation of cat hair and dog dander, but it didn't take away my bone weariness. Neither did a nap. I woke feeling lonely and uneasy. And because my mind is like a Scrabble game, in the next moment it was setting down old thoughts crossed by irrelevant thoughts butting up against tangential thoughts that somehow led to a sharp desire for Guidry like a slicing knife.

Before Guidry went away, I lay many nights thinking about all the reasons why my life would be less complicated without him in it. I counted them off like rosary beads. Then I would think of all the reasons why my body smiled when it was near him. More than likely, Guidry had been across town in his own bed counting the reasons his life would have been simpler without me — but his body must have smiled when I was around, too, because he kept coming back. We had been an odd couple, both of us on constant guard against getting cornered in a relationship but wanting and needing the intimacy and comfort it brings. Like two porcupines, we had kept our sharp quills on full alert but still came together to mate.

I sat up and stared at my bedside phone. Peter's voice sounded in my head: *Do you know now what you must do?*

He hadn't been talking about Guidry, but it was enough of a nudge to make me pick up the phone and dial Guidry's number.

He answered on the second ring. "Hi, Dixie." Caller ID has now made it impossible to surprise somebody with a phone call anywhere in the world.

I said, "I miss you."

A little voice in my head yelled, *No! No! You're supposed to be calling him to say you're going to go out with Ethan!*

Guidry's chuckle was a deep burr. I told the little voice in my head to shut up.

Guidry said, "Planes fly every day from Sarasota to Louis Armstrong Airport. Takes about four hours. Of course you'd have to miss seeing your pets while you were here."

There it was, that little cutting edge to his voice when he talked about pets. Guidry didn't particularly like pets. Ethan, on the other hand, had a dog he loved.

I said, "You're supposed to say, 'I miss you too, Dixie,' not give me flight schedules."

"I miss you too, Dixie."

He wasn't laughing. He really meant it.

I heaved a huge sigh. Judy was right, I was an idiot for letting Guidry leave without me. I was an idiot for not telling him the truth about Ethan. I was an idiot, period.

He said, "Do you ever take a vacation from pet sitting?"

I said, "Sure. You think I'm a robot?"

I grinned when I said it, meaning "I'm just joking," but the question had nettled me. The truth is that I haven't taken a vacation since I started pet sitting. In the beginning, I never took time off because I couldn't take the chance of all those empty hours with nothing to dam the river of pain and anger. Pet sitting was my escape. I could pour love into my charges and stifle the hatred I felt for the old man who'd killed Todd and Christy when he hit the gas pedal instead of the brake. I could discipline my mind by organizing my pet files and maintaining my pet-sitter insurance and making sure I observed all the professional ethics my pet-sitting organization required.

I could wash away the aura of anguish while I showered off cat hair and doggie drool. Work had been my salvation, and I couldn't let down my guard with a vacation.

After I got reasonably sane, I didn't take any time off because I didn't know what I'd do with myself if I did. There was no place I wanted to travel, no adventure I wanted to explore. At least not by myself. I might have liked a cruise in the cold seas around Alaska, but not alone. I might have liked to watch great blue whales, but not alone. I might have liked to go whitewater rafting or mountain climbing or kiss the Blarney Stone, but not alone. And I knew without asking that Guidry wasn't ready to go off and do any of those things with me. He might be ready later, but not now. Ethan, on the other hand, took annual vacations from his law office.

Guidry said, "What do you know about the murder in Cupcake Trillin's house?"

"You know about that?"

"Dixie, the entire world knows about that. Besides, Trillin's from around here, so everybody in New Orleans is especially interested."

Even to Guidry, I wouldn't repeat anything I'd just heard at Cupcake's house. Or tell him what Briana had told me. Or tell him about the men attacking me.

I could ask a question I'd been wondering about, though. "Guidry, do you know where Thibodaux, Louisiana, is?"

"Sure, that's where Trillin grew up. It's not far from New Orleans."

I should have remembered that sports fans know every detail of an athlete's history.

I said, "Do you remember anything about a sixteen-year-old Thibodaux girl killing a man? She shot him in the head and then disappeared. It would have been while Cupcake was in high school."

"This is Louisiana, Dixie. That kind of thing is common."

"Do you know anything about Serbian criminals?"

"Not a damn thing. Why?"

I laughed. "Because I don't either, and I wanted to make sure I wasn't the only ignorant one."

His voice took on a note of worry. "Dixie, you're not mixed up in something involving European criminals, are you?"

"Are you kidding? The only criminal I know is a cat who stole a slip of paper from a wastebasket. He's taken it to his lair, and he won't give it back."

"His *lair?* Cats have lairs?"

"Not all cats. Just criminal cats."

"I do miss you, Dixie."
"Those planes fly both ways."
"As soon as I can get away —"
"When might that be?"
"It's hard to say. There's so much to set straight here."

So there we were again, both of us putting something else first but promising to get together as soon as we could. It was the perfect time to say what was true: Neither of us would ever make that flight, because we had other things that took priority over getting together. But I couldn't say it. I wanted to, I tried to make my mouth form the words, but I flat couldn't. Some force I couldn't control wouldn't let me.

Instead, we murmured some more things, then ended the call. I sat staring at the phone for a moment, more frustrated and confused than ever. I had been a rank coward, merely putting off the inevitable, but Guidry had been an integral part of my coming out of the shell I'd crawled into after my husband and little girl died. He'd forced me to move on, to stop feeling sorry for myself, to let all the old anguish and resentment go and love again. While he'd been doing that, he'd let his own guard down and come to love me. To end what we had created together seemed to trivialize it, and it had not been trivial.

It had been a long dry spell without sex after my husband died, and making love with Guidry had been like adding water to Magic Rocks and watching them explode into glorious colors. I couldn't bear the thought of going back to a state of desiccation, but I also couldn't bear the thought of sex with men I didn't love. I didn't know if the lust I felt for Ethan might grow into love or remain a purely biological urge.

I got up and made a cup of tea. If I felt lonely and needy, it was my own fault. It occurred to me that I would make a fortune if I invented and patented a do-it-yourself create-a-man kit. It could be a large tablet that lonely women dropped in water. When it hit moisture, it would burst into the shape of a teeny man and then grow before their eyes into the exact man they needed.

I stood at the kitchen sink and drank my tea and grinned while I remembered reading a book in high school called *Gorilla, My Love.* In the book, a woman had explained to her sisters how a woman needed a lot of different men in her life. A lover man, a money man, a handy man, a smooth-talking, sharp-dressed man to take out in public, and a sweet, sensitive man for quiet evenings. I figured I could design my build-a-man kit with tablets that would create any one of those men. Women could keep the kits on hand and create the right man for any occasion.

The only problem I could see was that there'd have to be some system of disposing of one man when a woman was ready for another. No intelligent woman would create a man too dumb to know he was disposable, but it would be depressing to be with a man who knew his days were numbered.

The whole idea was beginning to seem like real life, so I rinsed out my cup and decided I would never get rich selling do-it-yourself man kits.

18

Before I left for my afternoon calls, Cora Mathers callcd. Cora is the eighty-something-year-old grandmother of a former client who was brutally murdered. The client had left a chunk of money to her grandmother and a significant sum to her cat named Ghost. Much to my dismay, she had named me the executrix of the cat's estate. But as it worked out, Cora thought it was cool that her granddaughter had left money to her cat, and I had found a good home for him. Tom Hale has invested the cat's money so wisely that he's a very rich cat. The rich part for me was that Cora and I have become good friends.

Her voice thin and scratchy, she said, "Dixie, I hate to bother you, but could you pick up something for me?"

She said she wanted a hot water bottle. Another woman in her condo had one, and just the thought of it had made Cora nostalgic for the hot water bottles she'd had when she was young.

She said, "They make them smaller now, so they're easier to handle. And there's nothing like a hot water bottle when you have a stomachache or when your feet are cold. The woman got hers at a drugstore on Tamiami Trail."

I said, "Do you have a stomachache?"

"It's not bad."

"Have you told your doctor?"

"It's not anything to worry about, Dixie. People get stomachaches."

I told her I'd be happy to bring her a couple of hot water bottles and hurried to get dressed so I could pick them up before I started my afternoon rounds.

Outside, the sun hid behind a scrim of ragged clouds, giving a trio of red-tailed hawks the look of dive bombers gone off course. The sun had moved away from dead center of the sky, making the light slant onto the ripples on the Gulf so their top edges glittered. A few sailboats made neat white triangles in the distance, and shore birds had come out of their siesta hideaways to stalk along the beach looking for snacks brought in with the frothy surf.

Michael was also on the beach, bare feet planted in the sand, legs braced like tree trunks while he looked at waves piling up on the shore. With a beach at our front door, we are generally considered privileged, but that only means we had ancestors smart enough or lucky enough to make choices that would one day be of tremendous value. Our grandfather bought our beachfront property for less than a thousand dollars. Now it's worth more than Michael's fire-fighting income and my pet-sitting income combined will ever total, but we still get to live here. If it's true that we choose our families, we chose well.

I slipped off my Keds and walked out on the beach to stand beside him and dig my toes into the sand's cool dampness.

I said, "What's wrong?"

He didn't pretend to be surprised that I knew something was wrong. We've been together a long time, and we know each other's moods.

"Just a little concerned about Paco. He's really stressed about something."

"A job?"

His voice grew sharp. "Of course a job. What else? And no, I don't know what job it is, and yes, it's none of my business so I'm not asking. He wouldn't tell me if I did."

I nodded. People with family members who do undercover police work are always a little bit anxious, a little bit worried, and a little bit resentful because we can't talk to them about it. They do their strong silent acts and we do our pretending-we're-not-worried acts, and sometimes those different acts create great swaths of distance between us.

I said, "I'm just guessing, but I think the homicide in the Trillin house was more than just a local murder. An FBI agent questioned me and the Trillins this morning. Not a *real* FBI agent, a guy on loan from Interpol. So whoever the murdered woman was, it has attracted international attention. I think Paco's involved in something to do with it."

Michael looked hopeful. "Interpol?"

I knew what he was thinking, that a murder investigation that attracted FBI agents and Interpol officers wouldn't be as dangerous for Paco as infiltrating a terrorist group or a local drug gang. It would be, of course, but I didn't burst his bubble. I told him I was going to buy Cora some hot water bottles and left him looking less stressed.

As I drove under the trees lining the lane, parakeets made friendly swoops from their leafy shelters and swirled overhead. Parakeets are prima donnas, but they earn it.

I stopped at the end of our lane and

waited for a break in traffic on Midnight Pass Road. As I turned, I caught sight of a white convertible half a mile away pulling out of a private lane like mine. It wasn't something I paid attention to, just one of those subliminal details that drivers notice.

I zipped to a Walgreens on Tamiami Trail and bought two hot water bottles for Cora. They were cuter than I remembered hot water bottles being. Sort of snuggly, actually, so I bought two for myself. I thought they might come in handy some chilly night when I had cramps or a backache or cold feet. Now that it looked like I would be sleeping alone for the rest of my life, I figured my feet might need something to keep them warm.

With the hot water bottles in tow, I sped off around the marina and its moored boats toward Cora's condo. Waiting at a red light, I spotted another white convertible way back in a line of cars behind me. It could have been a Jaguar like Briana's, but it was too far back to tell for sure. Lots of convertibles in Sarasota, many of them white. Nothing to pay attention to, really, but I sort of did. As I left the marina behind and followed Tamiami Trail to Cora's condo building, I noticed that the convertible hadn't turned to go over the bridge to

Longboat Key or St. Armands or Lido Key. When I turned onto the short lane to Cora's condo, though, the convertible went straight ahead on Tamiami Trail, headed north. I felt a ridiculous relief. Nothing like being involved in a murder investigation to make a person start imagining being followed.

Every time I look up at the condo building where Cora lives, I imagine a bunch of architects coming back from an inspiring but drunken weekend in Venice before they designed it. Instead of old-world charm, the building is tarted up so it resembles a giant wedding cake decorated by kindergartners let loose with frosting cones. Cupolas perch in weird places, columns soar without any purpose, little fountains spurt water from the lips of cherubic gargoyles. I get off balance just looking at it.

I pulled up under the porte cochere, and a valet trotted out to take my Bronco away. Well, he was too old to trot, but he moved as fast as possible. With so many retirees in Sarasota, most of our valet parkers and supermarket bag-boys are over seventy. I suspect that most of them have been pushed to it by wives who grew weary of them constantly underfoot. The Sarasota joke is that wives committed to their husbands for life, but not for lunch.

The valet who parked my car was new, so we didn't waste time chatting. I told him I wouldn't be long, grabbed the bag of hot water bottles, and scooted through wide glass doors that slid apart when they felt me coming. I like that about posh places. Even the mechanical objects make you feel special. The lobby was crowded with youthful gray-haired people headed to golf courses or tennis courts or movie theaters. Old people are the only people who have the time to enjoy themselves. Gives me something to look forward to.

The concierge waved at me from her French provincial desk and picked up her phone to alert Cora that I was on my way up. I like that about posh places. Even if they know you couldn't afford a down payment on the doormat, they treat you as respectfully as they treat the paying residents.

Most of the residents of Cora's building are the epitome of good taste and old money, but a woman with bright red hair teased out to Jesus was waiting for the elevator. She wore high heels, tight leggings, and a drapey top made for adolescents. Cosmetic surgery had pulled out all her wrinkles and sculpted her nose thin as a baby's finger bone, but when she turned to look at me, the eyes peering from under a fringe of red hair looked like the desperate eyes of an aging fox caught in a trap. I wondered if she'd had the surgeries hoping to snag a rich husband. Or maybe she'd had all the work solely for herself, just because she refused to look her age. Regardless of the reason, it didn't take a make over artist to know the woman had the same hunger for attention and love that makes unhappy teenagers draw heavy lines around their eyes and lips and trowel on thick makeup to cover every blemish. Not surprisingly, she reeked of cloying perfume.

Before the elevator opened for us, a handsome white-haired man rounded the corner. When he saw the woman, he came to a momentary stop with a look of panic on his face.

With an arch smile, she said, "There you are! You thought you could hide from me, didn't you! But now I've got you! You promised to come up and have a drink with me, and I'm not letting you slip away again!"

She had a prissy voice and held her too-red lips as if they were a pouch-purse with tight-pulled strings.

I could tell the gentleman felt cornered. But he smiled grimly, too polite to tell her to get lost, and allowed her to motion him into the elevator where he backed into a corner.

I followed them in, which made the woman turn round on me as if I had intruded into a private meeting.

With a haughty look at my shorts and the Walgreens bag in my hand, she said, "What is your business here, dear?"

The man looked sharply at her.

I smiled sweetly. "I'm going to see some gentlemen on the sixth floor. They're having a party."

I raised the Walgreens bag and waggled it so the hot water bottles shifted around. "I'm bringing interesting goodies!"

Her smile faltered, and her hand with its red talon fingernails rose as if she might clutch my shoulder to try to become my best friend.

The man's eyebrows rose and he pushed his spine closer to the wall, but his eyes were on the woman rather than on me. She was like a retriever on point, every inch of her quivering with excitement.

She said, "Who are they? Which apartment?"

I shook a playful finger at her. "Sorry, I'm not the kind of girl who spreads secrets."

The elevator stopped at the sixth floor, the doors opened, and I skipped out swinging my bag of hot water bottles. She leaned out to watch me until I turned and looked pointedly at her. As she removed her hand from the door so it would close, the man behind her grinned and gave me a friendly wave. I had the feeling he knew my bag didn't hold hot steamy sex toys. I also had the feeling he would not go with the woman to her apartment. I felt a little like a missionary who had saved somebody on the verge of making a big mistake.

For some fool reason, the woman in the elevator had made me think of Briana. Not the dyed red hair, because Briana's hair was expertly colored and looked natural. Briana didn't wear thick makeup, either, and I was sure that Briana was always dressed in elegant style. I wouldn't have been surprised if she'd had cosmetic surgery, but only because I assumed that women in her world did, not because she looked as if she'd had some work done. When I tapped on Cora's door, I was still trying to figure out why Briana's face had popped into my head while I looked at the woman in the elevator.

I heard Cora's thin voice raised to tell me to come in and forgot about Briana. Cora's pink and green apartment is lovely. Her granddaughter bought it for her with money she made in ways Cora has never suspected.

Cora was outside on the narrow terrace that runs the width of her apartment and affords a spectacular view of the bay. From her rattan peacock chair she could watch the constantly shifting blues, greens, lavenders, and grays of the bay under a clear blue sky. With natural vistas like Cora's, people in Sarasota don't need artwork on their walls.

With a weak smile, Cora watched me cross the apartment and step outside to the terrace. She was pale, with violet shadows under her eyes.

Alarmed, I said, "Are you okay?"

She waved a dismissive hand.

"I just did something stupid. Rose Tyler turned a hundred yesterday, and they always throw a big party for people on their hundredth. So I went down there to the ballroom, and nothing would do everybody but that I ate some of the cake. It was carrot cake, and I hate carrot cake. Always have. All that thick sweet stuff makes my teeth hurt. But I ate it anyway, because Rose will only be a hundred once, and I paid for it all night. Oh my, you wouldn't believe! I won't even tell you. I'm better now, but my stomach feels like it's not sure it wants to stay with me. I wouldn't be surprised if some other people had a problem with it, too. I think they'd let it sit out too long."

Relieved that she only had an upset stomach, and intending to have a word with the staff about that cake, I held up the Walgreens bag.

"I got your hot water bottles. Stay put, I'll fix them for you."

Cora usually has the teakettle on low all the time, but today nothing was going on in her one-person kitchen. I ran water into the kettle, and while it heated I got out tea things. I wasn't sure how hot the water for a hot water bottle should be, but I figured it shouldn't be boiling, so I filled the bottles before the kettle sang. I didn't fill them so much they bulged, just enough so the water made them firm. I poured the rest of the water from the kettle onto tea bags in Cora's little Brown Betty teapot and put it and two cups and saucers on a tray. With the hot water bottles individually wrapped in clean dish towels and stacked on one end of the tray, I carried the whole business out to Cora on the terrace.

She said, "I'm sorry I don't have any chocolate bread."

I was sorry, too. Cora makes sinful chocolate bread in an old bread-making machine her granddaughter bought her. She won't give her secret, but at some point in the bread-making process, she throws in bittersweet chips of chocolate. When the loaf is baked, it's dark and dense, and the chocolate chips are still soft and oozing. It's so good that I can't eat it without whimpering a little bit.

I said, "I'm just glad your tummy is better."

That was true, but as I arranged the towel-wrapped hot water bottles on Cora's tummy and handed her a cup of tea, it occurred to me that the disappointment of no chocolate bread after I'd got used to it was almost as depressing as no sex after I'd got used to it. That's probably why women with bad sex lives eat a lot of chocolate. If you can't have one, you turn to the other.

Being deprived of sex *and* chocolate is the pits.

19

I took one of the peacock chairs and tried to watch Cora without looking like I was watching. Cora gets testy if she thinks people are hovering over her. Her cheeks got a little pinker as she sipped her tea, and her eyes brightened.

I said, "Do you know a woman in the building with big red hair? She wears tight leggings and high heels."

Cora chuckled. "That would be Miss Taylor. She always comes down hard on the *Miss,* so all the men will know she's available. Poor soul, she never has settled into her own skin."

There it was, the thing that had reminded me of Briana.

"She was in the elevator with me. I sort of played a mean trick on her."

Cora's eyes brightened more when I told her how I'd given the impression I was a hooker going to a party of men on the sixth floor.

She said, "Oh my, that's wonderful. Except now she'll be hanging around on this floor looking for those men."

"At least I saved that man in the elevator from her clutches."

She rolled her eyes. "Men don't have the sense of fishing worms. Some of the men here follow that woman around like geese chasing somebody spilling seed on the ground. He should have just told her no."

I thought of Briana again. "I know a woman who reminds me a lot of Miss Taylor. She has something to do with fake merchandise."

She said, "Everything is fake nowadays. Fake butter, fake cheese, fake crabmeat, fake sugar. We've got a new activities director here, and he's got those colored contacts that are bigger than real eyes. His are bright turquoise. He looks like one of those people in that movie about giant people with a magic tree."

"Avatar?"

"Just like those people! And he doesn't seem to ever blink. He had a meeting where he told us all the new things he was planning for us, but I don't think anybody heard what he said. We were all watching those big turquoise eyes."

I said, "Maybe it's not fake if everybody knows it's fake."

"It's pitiful, is what it is. Everybody knows that man's real eyes aren't that big or that color, and everybody knows Miss Taylor isn't a young woman, so it's downright sad for them to think they're fooling people."

Thinking of all the fake people she knew had relaxed her face and removed the pain shadows from her eyes.

She said, "How's that young man of yours? The one you let go off to New Orleans without you?"

I responded like a springing rat trap. "Cora, Ethan Crane asked me out."

"Oh my, he's a nice-looking man. Looks a lot like his grandfather. I always wanted to know his grandfather better. I think he liked me, too, but he was too educated for me."

I'm always surprised to be reminded that old people are only old on the outside. Inside, they're the same age they were when they first started life as adults.

I said, "But I'm still involved with Guidry. At least I'm supposed to be. I talked to Guidry this afternoon, and I didn't tell him Ethan had asked me out. I meant to, but I just couldn't."

She turned eagle eyes on me. "Afraid to let one go before you decide if you want the other one?"

My face went hot. "It's not like that!"

"That's what it sounds like."

It sounded like an awful way to treat both men, and I didn't want to admit that Cora might be right.

She said, "Dixie, if you keep one foot in a boat and another on the dock, you'll be stuck in one place forever. If you want the first man, then for heaven's sake get your foot off the dock and go to New Orleans. If you can't do that, then get your foot out of the boat and stay here."

"I tell myself that all the time."

She smiled, the zillions of tiny lines in her face glittering in the sunlight. "Looks to me like your head says one thing and your feet say something else. You moon around about how much you miss that young man, but you're still here."

"It's complicated."

"Things are only as complicated as we decide to make them. Do you want to go out with Ethan?"

I groaned. "Yes."

"Then it's simple."

"I don't want to hurt Guidry."

"Has he come to see you since he's been gone?"

I didn't answer. She knew he hadn't.

"You want to know what I think?"

I didn't, not about this particular topic, but I knew I'd hear it anyway.

"I think he'll be as relieved to hear you're going to be seeing other men as you'll be to tell him. I imagine there are women in New Orleans he'd like to go out with. Women who *want* to live in that town."

"What if he starts seeing somebody there and I change my mind and want to go there and he doesn't want me anymore?"

She shrugged. "You take a risk when you love somebody."

I groaned again and slid forward in my chair like a frustrated kid.

For several minutes, we sat silently and let the sun seep into our bones. Until I'd said it, I hadn't realized my secret fear was that I might decide I wanted to be with Guidry and it would be too late. As Cora had said, I wanted to hedge my bets. I wanted to keep Guidry and at the same time explore other possibilities with a man like Ethan. I didn't need Cora to tell me that besides being dishonest and cowardly and manipulative, that was just plain *wrong.*

After a while, I sat up straight.

"Do you want to stay out here, or would you like me to help you inside?"

She thought about it, considered it from

all angles, and decided to go to bed with her hot water bottles and watch TV. I carried the bags and tea things inside, and while she went to the bathroom and got into a nightgown, I refreshed the hot water in the bags, put a bottle of mineral water on her bedside table, made sure her phone and TV remote were at hand, and helped her get situated against her pillows. In her white cotton nightie, she looked like a little girl.

I hugged her, kissed the top of her wispy hair, and made her promise to call me if her stomach started hurting again.

She said, "You're a good girl, Dixie. I hope you know that. You know, that may be why some people put on fake ways. Maybe they don't know they're good, so they try to make people think they're somebody else."

I blinked back sudden tears and hugged her again. Cora believes everybody in the world *came* good, no matter how they turned out. I don't know that I agree with her, but I'm glad she thinks I'm good.

Before I left her apartment, I peeked into the hallway to see if Miss Taylor was lurking about. She wasn't, but she got off the elevator before I got in it. She had changed into clingy black velvet pants and a sequined top.

Surprised to see me, she said, "Leaving so soon?"

I nodded. "Their wives are there, too. I didn't know there would be wives."

Her face fell, and she stepped back into the elevator with me. We rode down in heavily perfumed silence. I don't know what she was thinking, but I was giving silent thanks that she wasn't anything like my mother. My mother might have deserted me and my brother, but she would never look like Miss Taylor. It was nice to know I hadn't inherited bad-taste genes.

Downstairs, Miss Taylor turned with an air of resignation toward the activities room where people played cards and chatted before the dinner hour, which, in Sarasota, is five o'clock.

At the concierge desk, I stopped with a phony smile. "Ms. Mathers seems to have a touch of food poisoning from the carrot cake at the birthday party yesterday. I think she's going to be okay, but I'd appreciate it if you'd pass along a suggestion to your chef to refrigerate those cakes until they're served. We wouldn't want a resident to get seriously ill from one of them."

She wore colored contacts, too, but they weren't oversized. Her eyes rounded in alarm, and her gracious smile was just as phony as mine.

"We haven't had any other complaints. It

must have been something else Ms. Mathers ate."

"Could have been, but just to be on the safe side, I think it would be a good idea to keep an eye on her — but not so she *knows* you're keeping an eye on her."

This time the smiles we exchanged were genuine. Everybody at the retirement condo knew how much Cora hated being fussed over.

She said, "Somebody will check on her tonight. If she's not feeling well, we'll see that she goes to her doctor."

As I waited for the aged valet to bring my Bronco, I thought about how phoniness is so pervasive that we've come to take it for granted. Not just phony political rhetoric but phony smiles and phony conversations by ordinary people in which nobody says what they really think. With digital technology, photographs may have settings or people added or removed, and recordings of speeches or conversations may actually be random words spliced together to create a seamless whole. Most of us wear shoes and watches and jeans and T-shirts with fake labels in them, society matrons carry expensive handbags with fake labels, cigar aficionados puff pricey stogies with Cuban labels that are really from someplace else, and heroic athletic feats may be due to muscles or stamina falsely created by steroids. I wondered if living in a phony world changes the way our brains and cellular structures operate. If we accept phoniness, will we do away with honesty and integrity altogether? Will we make up new selves from day to day, with no obligation to mop up the messes the old selves have made? Most important of all, is it possible to be real in a phony world?

The rules of Cora's condo forbid tipping the valet, but I always tip anyway because I appreciate not having to lope around on the parking lot for my car. The new valet pocketed the money with a smile, and I drove away smiling back. I'm not sure if either of our smiles was genuine.

Everything in the world had begun to seem fake to me, so it was a huge relief to start making my afternoon pet rounds. If a dog wags its tail at you, he really means it. If a cat purrs at you, that's not a fake purr. And there's not a dog or cat in the world who would wonder if a change of eye color might make him more popular, or if dying her hair would bring her more attention. Animals may be the only creatures on earth who are content with being who they are.

I usually start at the south end of the Key

and work my way north, but since I was crossing the north bridge onto the Key, I changed my usual routine and called on two cats at the north end. They were sisters, sweet Siamese mixes named Gumdrop and Licorice. Young enough to find their primary entertainment in chasing each other through the house, they didn't let tile floors dampen their enthusiasm for racing. They slid and skidded a lot going around corners, but they seemed to find that an additional thrill.

When I unlocked their front door and went inside, I could hear the soft thudding noise of a wild galloping chase. The noise stopped when they heard me, and I called to them to set their minds at ease.

"It's just me, Dixie."

They came charging to look at me with that Siamese expression of alert intelligence. They followed me to the den, where I pulled a peacock feather from my bag. For a cat, a peacock feather waved over its head is an opportunity to leap into the air and grab a bird of its very own. For a cat sitter, waving a peacock feather over a couple of cats is an opportunity to sit on a hassock and enjoy watching the grace and style with which cats spring into the air. Since I had groomed them during the morning call, I was there solely to play with them and feed them.

With all the running they did, they got plenty of exercise on their own, but it's as good for cats to have new experiences as it is for humans.

The cats were fascinated with the feather, I was fascinated with the cats, and none of us knew Briana had come into the house until she was in the room with us.

20

I felt her before I saw her. A faint scent of perfume, perhaps, or just the rearrangement of the air's molecules by a foreign body. Curiously, I wasn't surprised. That white convertible I'd seen in traffic had really been following me, then, and a thief who knew how to disengage a specific area of a security system would surely have no trouble creating an electronic signal that would bypass a home's security pad.

Briana wore an outfit similar to the one she'd worn when we met at the beach pavilion — sheer, wide-legged white linen pants and a matching loose tunic. Not the *same* outfit, of course, just similar. Briana probably never wore the same clothes twice. Her silky red hair was twisted into a knot on the top of her head. Her hands hung loosely at her sides. She had glittering green stones in her ears, and I knew they were real emeralds. Briana wouldn't have been caught dead in fake emeralds.

I didn't even stop waving the peacock feather. The cats gave Briana a questioning look and went back to leaping at their prey.

I said, "When did they release you?"

"This morning. I told you I didn't kill that woman."

"But you knew who did."

She shrugged. "Justice will be done."

"I'm surprised they didn't hold you as a material witness."

"Thanks to you, I have a good lawyer who arranged bail."

"Why are you here?"

She sat down on the arm of a sofa.

"Dixie, I don't think you know the danger you're in. You're holding something that two groups of people much stronger than you want, and if you have any ideas about selling to the highest bidder, forget it. You're not dealing with sweet little pussycats, you're dealing with professionals who will snap you in half and throw your body into the ocean if you oppose them."

I lowered my right hand holding the feather and let my elbow rest on my knee. My gun was in the right pocket of my cargo shorts, and I wanted to be ready to grab it. The peacock feather was still suspended in the air but not moving. The cats watched it suspiciously.

I said, "What is it that you think I have?"

"I must have dropped it in Cupcake's bedroom and you found it." With an arch smirk, she added, "If you were the law-abiding citizen you claim to be, you would have turned that list of contacts over to the FBI."

I thought, *List of contacts?*

I moved the peacock feather to my left hand and waggled it. The cats jumped at it. Briana watched the cats while I slid my right hand up my thigh to the flap of the pocket on my cargo shorts. I hooked my thumb in my pocket as if I were resting my hand.

I said, "Why should I give you the list, Briana?"

Her mouth made a little O of realization.

"You want to be my partner? My Florida agent? Is that it?"

"Maybe."

Her lips curled. "I've worked my butt off to get where I am. I've been felt up by every obnoxious old fart in Europe. Plus, I can't take a pee without some goddamn paparazzi catching me on film. You think you can just waltz in and share in the profits when all you've done is find a list of names?"

I swirled the peacock feather in the air with my left hand while my right hand slid all the way into my pocket and grasped the butt of my .38.

I said, "I know you had to work hard to be who you are. I really admire that."

Oddly, I actually meant it.

She said, "You wouldn't believe all the people in the fashion world that top models have to kiss up to. Not to mention rich men who think a model is just an expensive whore."

I said, "Like the Serbian gangster who went to prison for adding heroin to a shipment of fake Gucci watches?"

Her eyes widened, and I was afraid I'd gone too far. Then she laughed. "I guess my life is more of an open book than I'd realized."

In my pocket, I laid my trigger finger alongside the barrel of the gun.

She said, "You know, the partnership you're proposing might be a good idea. You have the right contacts for my business. They're all around you. Some of them are probably your clients. Since you already know what the business is, perhaps we should talk about how we might help each other."

"You'd cut me in on your profits if I help you?"

"Right."

"Doggone generous of you, considering that I'm the one with the list of names."

Briana said, "The list is only one side of the equation. I hold the other side. One without the other is useless."

I had pushed my luck as far as it would go. If I made one slip, Briana would figure out that I really didn't have a list of names. I didn't even know why the names were important, but I was pretty sure they had something to do with an illicit business involving fake designer merchandise.

I said, "I still don't understand why you stalked Cupcake."

Her eyes closed, and for a second she looked like an ancient carving. Gumdrop must have felt her sadness, because she jumped onto the sofa and nuzzled Briana's arm with her nose. Briana opened her eyes, smiled, and began to stroke Gumdrop's head.

She said, "Cupcake was the sweetest boy I ever knew. He didn't have a mean bone in his big muscle-bound body. After I killed my uncle, somebody told the cops that I had a hideout in the swamps. I didn't, and I'd never told anybody I did, but while I was losing myself in the French Quarter, search parties were slogging through every bayou and swamp in the county. I always suspected Cupcake was the one who told that swamp story."

"So to pay him back for his kindness, you broke into his house?"

"I've already told you why I did that. I just wanted to be close to him again. He's one of the few people in the world who's truly good. I needed to have some of that goodness, even if it was just from hanging around his house."

"Who was the woman who was killed?"

"The FBI agent? I don't know her name."

I tried not to look surprised, but it was hard. Mostly, I felt stupid. Now I understood why the murdered woman's identity had been kept a secret, and why Paco was involved in the investigation.

"Who killed her?"

"I don't know."

"I don't believe you."

She shrugged. "Will you help me or not?"

"Who were the men who attacked me and searched my apartment?"

She looked surprised. "I didn't know that happened. But now that I do, I can tell you they were business rivals of mine. They want that list you have."

"Well, isn't that just peachy."

"Will you help me?"

"Tell me about the list."

"My old Serbian friend passed them along to me before he went to prison. He wanted me to carry on his business until he got out. Since he was murdered in prison, the business is now wholly mine."

"And the rivals? How do they know about the names?"

She looked uncomfortable. "They were my friend's partners. They expected to take over the business while he was in prison."

"Only you took it from them instead."

"My friend wanted me to have it."

"Is that why he was killed in prison?"

She smiled and shrugged. "It's a cruel business, Dixie."

Images flitted across my mind like a slide show: Briana in her designer clothes slouching down a runway, the counterfeit black Nikes left on Cupcake's bed, the murdered woman's bloodstained white shirt.

"Did you get the reward money for turning in your Serbian gangster friend?"

She looked surprised again, as if I were a frog she'd picked up that was turning into a prince.

"That was for *money,* it wasn't personal. I saw the opportunity and I took it."

Even Gumdrop and Licorice looked shocked.

She said, "I know what you're thinking,

but models only have a few good years, and most of us aren't lucky enough to marry a Sarkozy or a Mick Jagger or a Billy Joel. We have to think of our future."

"Explain to me exactly how your business works."

She looked bored. "Counterfeit goods are manufactured in Asian countries, China mostly, and shipped out under fake papers showing them originating in Croatia or Montenegro or some other Balkan country. The American shipment is stored in a warehouse in New Jersey, then distributed to shops in big-money resort areas. The shop owners buy at a big discount and sell at a large markup."

"How do you solicit those shop owners?"

She smiled. "That's the tedious part. It took my friend years to build up his stable of upper-crust retail outlets. He did it himself, not like some who hire people to do it. He traveled to every store in person, and each place he went he had a different disguise, a different name. He was a master at disguise. He told people he was an agent for the manufacturer, and for one retailer he'd put on a wig and beard, then go bald and with fake teeth to call on the next. He was good with words, too. He'd get people talking, and when he left nobody could remember exactly what he looked like."

For a second, I had a disastrous urge to laugh. A slick criminal had spent years building a list of secret markets where his counterfeit goods were sold. When he was arrested, he had double-crossed his partners by giving the list to a sexy model — the same sexy model who had turned him in to the police for the reward. The man had been killed in prison for his double-cross, and the sexy model had come to Florida to introduce herself to the retailers on the list, expecting to carry on the business and make billions. But because she had come to believe in a false memory she'd created of being Cupcake's close friend when they were sixteen, she'd broken into his house. While she was inside, she'd lost the list. A transnational counterfeit business had been thrown into disarray because of a false memory and a woman's carelessness.

I said, "You know, you could have saved yourself a lot of grief if you'd made a copy of that list."

She looked ashamed. "I'm not used to the clerical end of business."

I felt a stab of pity. With no family, Briana had been forced to create herself, and the self she'd created was truly amoral. With her blend of nuttiness and slyness, life was a game to her, a chance to become involved in intrigue and manipulation of other people. Her sense of self was so slippery that she broke into other people's houses to see how normal people lived. She was obsessed with Cupcake for the same reason she'd been obsessed with her Serbian gangster friend: They both exuded power and self-confidence. Reba Chandler had been right about Briana's addiction to drugs released by danger. Getting the list of contacts had been so scarily satisfying to her that she hadn't given any thought to the practical, mundane, ordinary ways that people held on to important papers. Instead of making a copy of her precious list, she'd carried it around the same way Elvis carried his pilfered papers.

Cupcake had been right about Briana, too. The woman had a bag of unusually lustrous marbles, but she wasn't playing with all of them.

I pulled my hand away from my gun. Briana was dishonest and cunning, but she wasn't a physical danger.

I said, "Somebody told me that you did something outrageous at the Milan fashion show last year. What was that about?"

Her eyes rounded in surprise again. "One of the men trying to take over my business was in the audience. He made a gesture toward a reporter, a way of telling me he was going to expose me. He wouldn't have, of course, because he would have been exposing himself at the same time, but the threat made me furious. I leaped off the runway and beat at him with my fists. It got me good publicity because I told the reporters he had made an obscene gesture that I found highly offensive. I was the injured innocent." With a world-weary roll of her eyes, she said, "That's the way it is in this business. The competition is cutthroat."

"Aren't you afraid of being caught?"

She shrugged. "My modeling career would be ruined, but I'm close to a time when I'll have enough money to live without sucking up to prime ministers and wealthy playboys."

She sounded as if she were talking about grabbing a bargain at Marshalls.

Suddenly defensive, she said, "I'm not the only famous person selling copies of top fashions and distributing them under fake labels. It's a way to make millions, and the risk isn't great. If someone is caught bringing in a container of fake sneakers, they lose their goods and get a mark on their customs records, but that's all. It's not like getting caught with three kilos of coke in a shipment of Gucci watches like my friend did. That was a stupid thing to do, because it gets you a four-year prison sentence. I'd never do that."

I heaved a huge sigh and stood up. The cats circled around me eying the peacock feather that was now at my shoulder height.

"Briana, you have to leave now. These cats have to be fed, and then I have other pets to call on. Don't follow me, and don't come in another house after me."

Confusion moved across her face like spiderwebs. "What about the list?"

"I run a business, Briana. Business people make copies of important papers. I've made several copies of your list. One of the copies is in my safety deposit box at the bank. If anything should happen to me, the list will go to every newspaper editor and law enforcement agency in Florida."

She shook her head. "What are you saying?"

"I'm saying to leave me the hell alone. Leave me alone, leave Cupcake alone, leave his wife alone. We are not a part of your world, and we don't want to be. And if you're in contact with your rivals, pass the word along to them. If they come after me again, that precious list of contacts will be spread all over the world."

I left her sitting on the arm of the sofa and went to the kitchen, where I fed the cats and gave them fresh water. When I went back to the den, Briana was gone.

21

Sometimes being a good pet sitter means that you do the same thing a good parent does: You fake it. You pretend that everything is fine and dandy, that everything is normal, that there's nothing to get anxious about, when all the time your knees are trembling and your tongue is cottony with abject panic. But children and animals always know when you're lying, so even though I pretended to be calm when I told Gumdrop and Licorice good-bye, their eyes said they knew better and their ears pointed forward in a show of uneasiness. Briana had not only scared the bejesus out of me, she'd caused me to upset the cats. The woman seemed to create discord and destruction everywhere she went.

By the time I arrived at the next client's house, my whirling mind had arrived at a plan. I parked in the driveway and called Cupcake from my cell.

I said, "I don't have time to go into all the details now, but please call Steven and ask him to meet me at your house in three hours. Tell him I have a list of local businesses selling counterfeit designer goods."

"You do?"

"Well, sort of. I'll explain when I see you."

I galloped through the rest of the pet visits, looking over my shoulder before I went into every house, listening for footsteps while I played with cats. I didn't expect Briana to come after me again. She had nothing to gain from accosting me again if I had copies of the list of contacts, and she'd looked as if she believed me when I said I did. But I wasn't sure the men with the sap and the asp baton would be as easy to manipulate. If Briana had sent a message to them that I'd made copies of their stupid list, they might kill me just out of spite.

Since I had reversed my usual pattern and started at the north end of the Key, Billy Elliot was my last call instead of my first. He and Tom were waiting for me with anxious faces.

I said, "I'm sorry I'm so late. I had to take some hot water bottles to Cora Mathers, and since I was coming from the north end, I worked my way south."

Tom watched me snap Billy Elliot's leash

on his collar. "How is Ms. Mathers?"

"She ate some carrot cake that gave her a tummy ache."

"She's a nice lady."

What he meant was that Cora was an innocent lady. Tom handles Cora's finances, and he knows as well as I do that the money her granddaughter left her didn't come from shrewd investments the way Cora thinks. It came from a clever blackmailing scheme that was never exposed because the granddaughter was murdered. I appreciate Tom's discretion in the way he keeps Cora innocent. She's had too many hard knocks in her life to learn this late that her beloved granddaughter was a phony.

Billy Elliot and I went downstairs, and as soon as he had peed on every bush that needed peeing on and had run around the oval track three times, I took him back upstairs. Tom was sitting in his wheelchair with an anxious face.

"Dixie, you don't have to tell me anything if you don't want to, but I know something is wrong. If you're in any trouble that I can help you with, please don't do a strong stoic act. I'm your friend, and friends help friends."

My eyelids pricked with hot tears. Sometimes I get so overwhelmed with the rank awfulness of parts of the world that I forget we're all connected by a solid foundation of goodness and kindness.

I stooped to remove Billy Elliot's leash before I answered him. I was afraid I'd bawl like a baby if I talked before I got myself under control. Billy Elliot caught the atmosphere and looked from Tom to me with a quizzical arch to his eyebrows.

I said, "I can't talk to you about it yet, but as soon as it's over, I'll tell you all about it."

"Are you in danger?"

I hesitated. "Maybe."

"Have you called Guidry?"

There it was, the reminder that my protector was gone. For a moment, I felt a stab of annoyance, a woman's resentment that a man thought she needed another man to keep her safe. But the truth was that I was up against an amoral woman with transnational criminal contacts, not to mention a rogue security cadre who answered to no recognized authority. Both groups believed I possessed information vital to their existence, and neither of them would hesitate to use torture to get what they wanted.

I said, "I'm meeting in just a few minutes with an FBI agent."

"This has something to do with that woman killed in Trillin's house, doesn't it?"

I nodded. "The woman was an FBI agent. That's all I can tell you now."

Tom had gone pale. "Somebody killed an FBI agent in Cupcake Trillin's house? Good God."

Tom's smart. I could almost hear the gears in his brain processing the implications of an FBI agent being in Cupcake's house while an internationally famous model was there, too, and what the agent's murder might mean.

He said, "Will you let me know if there's anything I can do?"

"I promise."

I left with a fake cheery smile and assurances that I was being very careful and that everything was going to be fine, but I wasn't sure that everything was going to be fine at all. I'd had a sample of the Serbian group's ability to inflict great pain without leaving evidence, and it scared me. I don't like pain. I don't deal well with pain. If I were tortured, I'd probably confess everything in about three nanoseconds. If I did, they would move to Cupcake's house and do God-knew-what to get that list.

Before I drove out of Tom's parking lot, Michael called to tell me he was going to an Orioles/Mets spring training game at Sarasota's Ed Smith Stadium, so he wouldn't be home for dinner. I was sorry he wouldn't make dinner but glad he wouldn't be home to see all the emotions I was feeling. I didn't want him to know anything about my fear of men coming with saps to hurt me, because he would go ape-shit if he knew it had happened before. When Michael feels the call to protect me, he tends to break bones.

I arrived at Cupcake's house almost exactly three hours from the time I'd called and told him to have Steven there. A brown sedan was parked in Cupcake's driveway, so Steven had apparently taken my message seriously. Before I got out of the Bronco, I got my gun from my shorts pocket and put it in the glove compartment. Friends don't carry guns into friends' houses.

When I rang the bell, Jancey opened the door. She looked annoyed, scared, and angry. I didn't blame her. She had gone to bed one night the wife of a famous athlete who was admired by everybody who knew him and woken up the next morning the wife of a famous athlete whose reputation was teetering on the razor's edge of disaster.

She said, "What's going on, Dixie?"

"Do you have a ladder?"

"A ladder?"

"I need to climb up to look in the cats'

hiding places."

She opened her mouth to ask a question, then closed it and hurried ahead of me to the kitchen where Cupcake and Steven sat drinking coffee.

"Cupcake, Dixie needs a ladder."

Both men looked up at me as if Jancey had asked for a flying saucer, but Cupcake lumbered to his feet and went through the kitchen door to the garage. Steven stood up and looked a question at me. I waited until Cupcake came back carrying a stepladder so long the ends of it waved out of control. Jancey rushed to support the ends, not because Cupcake couldn't handle the weight but because she didn't want her walls scratched.

Without waiting for them, I turned and moved rapidly toward the media room.

Steven said, "What are you doing, Ms. Hemingway?"

"Elvis has stashed a paper in one of the condos on the climbing tree."

"Excuse me?"

The outraged disdain in his voice was palpable. It said he was an important man with an important case to solve and I was wasting his time looking for a scrap of paper a cat had hidden.

I whirled so fast that Jancey jerked her

end of the ladder and bumped it against the wall.

I said, "You know, I've had it with you guys! You waltz in here with your leather jacket and your beard thing, and you let me think you're a homicide detective when you're really an FBI agent but you're just on *loan* as an FBI agent because you're really with Interpol, and you investigated us and you questioned us and you warned us that we're in danger, and in the meantime *I'm* the one who got worked over with a sap and *I'm* the one who was stalked by Briana, and you and your leather jacket didn't do a damn thing to protect me. Now I'm here to solve your case for you and you have the unmitigated audacity to question what I'm doing! Talk about a weenie thinking it's a salami! Please, please, please just shut the hell up and let me get the evidence you need so the rest of us can get on with our lives!"

His green eyes met mine, and a spark of humor took the place of outrage. "I beg your pardon. Please show me the evidence."

I knew he meant it as an apology, but I didn't forgive him. I was tired of the whole thing. I wanted to be done with Briana and her sordid enterprise.

In the media room, the humans clustered

together and watched me scan the places the cats used for hiding or sleeping. The cat condos were at different levels on the climbing tree, all covered in soft fuzzy fabric, each a different size and color. They looked a bit like a cluster of colorful houses clinging to a Mediterranean hillside.

Without speaking, I motioned to Cupcake to bring the ladder forward. He obeyed as silently as I had flapped my hand. I had become the imperious director of a play, and all the stagehands moved at my command. I pointed to the spot where I wanted the ladder set, and Cupcake carefully spread its legs and made sure it was secure for me to climb.

Figuring I'd begin with the easiest ones, I had chosen a fat turquoise condo on a lower limb of the tree. I could get to it by climbing only four or five rungs of the ladder. When I looked inside, I saw a felt mouse and a single strand of heavy string. I climbed down and motioned Cupcake to move the ladder. The next short tube was ruby red. It must have been a favorite spot of Lucy's, because it held a nice supply of white cat hair. Otherwise, it was completely empty. I pointed at another wide tube, Cupcake repositioned the ladder, and I climbed up again. This time I found paper, but it was a grocery store receipt, not the paper I wanted.

Jancey and Steven stood silently watching while Cupcake and I went through our routine. I motioned where I wanted the ladder, he moved it, I climbed up and peered inside a condo, then climbed down, and we repeated the whole process with another tube.

Twenty feet above us, Elvis and Lucy watched from their racetrack at the ceiling. The track had padded sides to keep them from accidentally slipping off while they bounded after each other, so we could only see their heads and wide eyes looking down at us. Maybe it was my imagination, but they seemed to be offended that I was snooping into their napping and hiding places. I didn't blame them.

I prayed that Elvis hadn't dropped the list on the racetrack. Getting up that high and inspecting every foot of the track would take people with more experience and taller ladders than I had.

I was mentally thumbing through the names of painters and paperhangers I knew when I climbed to the top rung of the ladder and looked into a bright orange tube. A crumpled slip of thin paper lay pushed against one side, as if a cat had napped with the paper against his back. Holding my breath, I reached inside and pulled the paper out. About six inches long and four inches wide, it had been folded and stuffed in a handbag, held between a cat's teeth, laid upon, and pushed between a cat's body and the side of the tube. It held the imprint of feline incisors, and the ink was blurred by cat spit, but the names, addresses, and phone numbers were legible. I recognized some of the names of upscale stores where wealthy tourists shop when they come to southwest Florida.

I looked up at Elvis, who was fixing me with the steely-eyed look of a department store detective about to make an arrest.

"Sorry, Elvis."

Clutching the list with the same determination with which Elvis had held it, I climbed down the ladder. I held the paper out to Steven.

"These are Briana's local contacts. I'm sure she has a similar list for other cities, but this is the one she and her rivals thought I had. She had it in her handbag when she broke in here to leave the Nikes on the bed. The cat got it and took it up to his hiding place on the climbing tree. Briana's former boyfriend gave the list to her before he went to prison. His partners saw that as a betrayal, so they had him killed. Their security people knocked me out because they thought I had the list."

Steven took the paper and gave it a cursory glance. "How do you know this?"

"Briana came in one of the houses where I was pet sitting. She offered to cut me in on her business because she thought I had the list of merchant names. She had the counterfeit merchandise, so she thought we could be partners. I told her I had made multiple copies of the list and that I would make them public if anybody leaned on me."

He nodded as if he approved. I didn't care.

I said, "This has to stop, Steven, and it has to stop now. The stalking, the assaults, the home intrusions. You're the law enforcement officer here, not me. So stop all this."

Steven opened a small notebook, carefully laid the list of names inside it, and closed it.

"Two details still to be answered, Ms. Hemingway: Why the Nikes on the bed, and who killed the woman?"

"Like I said, Steven, it's *your* job to figure those things out, not ours. Briana told me the woman was an FBI agent. I assume that means your people were already watching Briana before the murder."

Cupcake said, "They must not have been

watching very well."

Steven flushed, and I realized that humiliation was part of the reason the FBI hadn't released the murdered agent's name. Cupcake was right. They hadn't protected one of their own, and she'd been murdered.

Steven said, "Ms. Hemingway, did Briana say anything about the murder?"

"She claims she doesn't know who did it. I didn't press her on it."

"So how did your meeting end?"

"I told her to leave me alone, and to leave Cupcake and Jancey alone."

"That's it?"

"That's it. She left, and I finished my rounds and came here."

"How did you know where you'd find the list?"

I shrugged. "I know Elvis. He has a paper fetish."

He looked as if he doubted that a cat could have a fetish of any kind but wisely kept quiet about it. He thanked me for giving him the list, apologized to Cupcake and Jancey for the inconvenience they'd endured, and went off in his nondescript brown sedan to do FBI things.

Cupcake and Jancey and I said exhausted good-byes, and I went off in my Bronco to find solace in my apartment. I didn't see them do it, but I'd bet good money that Elvis and Lucy bounded down to snuggle into their favorite roosts on the climbing tree. Whether you're a cat or a human, nothing makes you feel as safe as the comfort of a soft enclosure.

22

I should have felt enormous relief, but I didn't. I was glad I'd found the precious list that Briana had left in Cupcake's house, and glad I'd given it to an FBI agent. Now he knew which store owners in the area were knowingly selling fraudulent merchandise and charging for the real thing. Of course, targeting retailers and arresting them for selling fake merchandise was only half the solution. The other half was arresting Briana for providing the merchandise, and there was no proof the list had come from Briana.

Except for breaking into Cupcake's house, there was no absolute proof of any criminal act that involved Briana. She hadn't been charged with the agent's murder. She hadn't even been held in jail as a material witness. Either the homicide officers believed she was completely innocent of any knowledge of the crime or they were waiting for her to lead them to the killer. There was a good likelihood that she would walk away with only a fine for breaking and entering. She would return to Rome or Paris or wherever she lived and continue to run a business that manufactured fake designer merchandise.

Even more depressing was the fact that the person who had killed the FBI agent in Cupcake's house would probably never be identified or apprehended. I didn't believe Briana's claim that she had disengaged one section of the security system for only the time it took her to enter the house. I thought it was more likely that she had left it disengaged the entire time she was inside. The security people wouldn't have noticed that one small section was switched off, so the security cameras that should have captured photos of Briana, the FBI agent, and the killer entering the house would have been inoperative.

Law enforcement people don't like to talk about it, but every police department and sheriff's office has files of homicides in which somebody literally got away with murder. Most homicides are committed by people with whom the victim has some connection. A rejected lover, a disgruntled employee, a jealous husband or wife, people whose emotional barometer went kaflooey one day and sent them into a self-pitying rage that ended with another person's death. Those killers leave a trail, either a physical trail or a historical one. But when the victim is a law enforcement officer and there are no witnesses or trace evidence left behind, the hunt for the killer becomes highly problematic.

While my mind chased after all the loose ends of the entire Briana situation, a solemn voice in my head asked, *What is that to you?*

I didn't have much of an answer. As long as nobody attacked me or stalked me, none of it had anything to do with me. Oh, I could drum up some righteous indignation about people stealing designers' ideas and selling them as originals instead of the knockoffs they really were, and I deplored slavelike conditions forced on workers in factories churning out fake designer products, but my supply of righteous indignation can only stretch so far, and there were plenty of things closer to home to get riled up about.

Even the FBI agent's murder was an objective fact to me, not something that engaged my private emotions. I was sorry it had happened, but sorry in the way I was sorry when I read about the murder of any other person I didn't know. Sorry I belonged to a species that includes beings who have lost their minds and souls to such an extent they can destroy another being. Sorry for the anguish the victims' deaths caused their families and friends, sorry for the anguish the killer's family and friends suffered. But the sadness wasn't personal. It didn't change *my* life. No matter how awful I thought the whole thing was, my sadness wouldn't bring the agent back to life, and my disgust wouldn't stop some people from cheating other people. Maybe it was pure self-centered selfishness on my part, but my main feeling was that I hoped I never saw Briana again.

At the entrance to my lane, I stopped at the row of mailboxes to pick up mail. I riffled through it and tossed the entire lot into the passenger seat to transfer to the recycle bin under the carport. Most of it was junk mail or ads from posh stores promoting expensive jewelry or designer clothing like outrageously pricey jeans. I made a scornful snort at a photo of a curvy model wearing designer jeans. Even if they were real and not counterfeit, jeans exist to make a woman's butt look good, and cheap jeans do the trick as well as expensive jeans.

Driving slowly so as not to alarm the

parakeets in the trees overlooking my lane, I could see wind surfers on the bay and hear the waves moaning before they slapped the shore. Overhead, a scrawl of white and black gulls wheeled against a clear blue sky. On the beach, little sandpipers scurried back and forth on the sand like kindergartners at recess. Through the open car window I could hear the twittering of songbirds in the trees and the sad lament of a mourning dove somewhere in the distance. I was back in my own world, and for the moment I could forget everything about Briana.

Rounding the curve to the carport, I saw that Michael's car was gone, and so was Paco's. A small branch had fallen from one of the oak trees beside the carport and landed on the shell in front of Michael's parking spot. Old oaks drop branches like that, sort of like a cat shedding hair. I pulled into my own spot and slid out of the Bronco, looking at the branch for the best place to grab it to throw it out of Michael's way. It was about the thickness of a baseball bat, around five feet long, with a multitude of leafy twigs at its end.

I stooped to grasp it somewhere around its middle. As my fingers closed around it, I heard a scuffling noise in the shell. I turned my head to look toward it and saw a pair of black-clad legs running toward me. Jerking upward, I swiveled toward the running figure, and my move caused the leafy end of the branch to scrape across Lena's outstretched hand. The twigs caught the hypodermic needle in her fingers and flipped it to the ground.

From the corner of my eye, I caught a spot of red at the edge of my porch. Looking up, I saw a pair of long milky white legs in bright red high-heeled pumps. The legs were sprawled at the top of the stairs.

Lena made a guttural sound and moved away from the branch, but she continued to come toward me, and she held a long knife in her hand. The knife flashed silver in the sunlight, but its cutting edge was stained wine red. She leaped toward me, her teeth glittering like the knife. In seconds, I was in a fight for my life.

Curiously, a red curtain seemed to descend over the world. Through the red haze, I realized that Lena was determined to kill me. The hypodermic needle had been intended to inject something into me to make me immobile while she slit my throat with her knife. Without the needle, she had to overpower me. Lena was hard and wiry and mean, but sheer terror gave me a burst of strength.

I kicked toward the knife and felt a searing pain in my ankle. Blood rushed onto my white Keds, and Lena smiled. Holding the branch with both hands, I swung it at her. I wiped the smile off her face, but she still had the knife, and my ankle was cut badly enough to fill my shoe with blood.

Irrationally, I thought how awful it would be for Michael and Paco to come home and find me dead in the yard.

I swung the branch again, and while Lena was adjusting her stance, I managed to swing it back the opposite direction. The second swing took her by surprise, so I kicked at the knife again. This time I connected. The knife flew out of her hand, and her head raised with a shocked glare. We both dived for the knife. I got to it first, but before I could stand up with it, she fell on me and her arm circled my neck in a steel vise.

Facedown, I clutched the knife under my midriff, but my victory had become a defeat. With her arm so hard against my throat that I feared the hiatal bone would break, I knew there was a good chance that Lena would strangle me to death.

Dimly, I heard the sound of a car racing to a stop nearby, then running footsteps crunching across the shell.

A man's voice shouted, "It is finished! Let her go!"

Lena screamed, "Fool, she has the list!"

I felt a struggle above me, and then Lena's arm slipped away from my throat and my face fell forward into the shell. A second later, Lena's weight left my back, and I scrambled to a sitting position with bits of shell sticking into my flesh. My heart was racing, my ankle was pouring blood, and my nose was leaking.

Lena crouched a few feet away, her face twisted into a grimace of pure hatred. Peter held a gun to Lena's temple. He looked resolute and devastated.

Peter said, "It's over, Lena. Too many people have been destroyed."

Lena said, "You are a fool, Peter. You have always been a fool."

They both spoke English, as if they were speaking to each other through me.

Through my ruined lips, I said, "I gave the list to the FBI."

Lena inclined her head toward my stairs. "*She* said you made copies of it. I want those copies."

"I lied when I told her that. There are no copies. The FBI agent has the only copy that existed."

"I don't believe you."

"Call the FBI and ask. I have the agent's number on my phone. Would you like to call him?"

Peter made a slashing motion with his hand. "I said *it's over!*"

Lena said, "You do not decide what is over and what is not over! That is for me to decide!"

I struggled into a more comfortable position against the carport wall and looked toward Briana's body. I wondered if the blood came from a vein or an artery.

I said, "Is Briana dead?"

Lena nodded with no more emotion than she would have shown if I'd asked if a plant needed watering.

"You killed her?"

"She ruined my business."

"The counterfeit business was *yours?*"

She raised her head proudly. "The company that manufactures the merchandise is mine. You think that stupid woman could have run a company like mine? No brains, no business mind, no sense! Who takes a pair of shoes and leaves them on a man's bed? I ask you, who? A crazy, stupid woman bringing down the police on our heads, that's who! And who breaks into a house when she knows the police are watching her? If I had not saved the fool, we would all have been caught!"

I said, "You killed the FBI agent, too. You injected a muscle paralyzer into her and then slit her throat."

"Who else? I could not trust my weak husband to do it. Like everything else, I had to do it myself. Men are fools! Soft, stupid fools like pretty women!"

Peter made a soft sound, as if he swallowed a sob.

I tried to remember what I'd been taught in the police academy about talking to irrational people.

"It must have been very difficult to kill that agent and get away so quickly."

She looked proud. "I didn't make a sound. I'm good at that. I slipped in the door the fool had left unlocked, and I moved through the house. But you had already come and spoiled it all. After you left, she ran to put on clothes. She was like a chicken, no brains. I waited to guide her to the car where Peter waited like a faithful dog. But the other woman came in the same way I had, through the back, her badge and guns ready to arrest Briana, arrest me, ruin our work and our lives. She was a fool, too, to come alone. She was arrogant, wanted the glory of the arrest without assistance from her colleagues. She never saw me before I killed her."

"So Briana lied when she said she didn't know who killed the woman."

Lena smiled grimly but didn't answer.

As if he had to give Lena deserved credit, Peter said, "Briana's only talent is dishonesty."

Lena said, "I stripped the agent of all identifying evidence and fled — but stupid Briana had let the list fall from her handbag. Stupid, stupid, stupid!"

His voice heavy with sadness, Peter said, "Lena, I don't know the woman you have become. You have lost sight of our reason for being. You have become the thing we always hated, the greedy, dishonest, murderous people we've fought all our lives."

Lena gave him a withering look that held an ambitious woman's scorn for a less ambitious man. With no warning, he fired his gun. Lena's head flew apart, her torso snapped backward, one arm flying up, her knees crumpling. Odd how the body reacts before the first drop of blood has time to leave the body, as if it feels the shock of death even before its spirit has left. As her body hit the ground, I felt a stab of pity.

Wailing, Peter fell on her body, cupping himself around her like a lover. His gun had fallen. I scrabbled to my knees and crawled to the branch. I broke off a sturdy twig, crawled to the gun, and slipped the twig through the trigger ring so I could lift it without touching it. Like a three-legged cat, I crawled to the Bronco with Peter's gun hanging from one hand. At the Bronco, I managed to hoist myself up on one leg and reach to the glove box and get my own gun.

The red haze had returned in front of my eyes, and my fingers trembled when I got my cell phone from my pocket and dialed 911.

I gave my name and address and said, "I want to report two murders. Both killers are on the scene. One is dead."

"Are you in danger, ma'am?"

I looked at Peter's quivering form holding Lena as if she were his lifeline.

"No, but I have a deep cut on my leg and I'm losing a lot of blood."

"Help is on the way."

I ended the call and everything went black.

I woke up to the sound of sirens and the feel of hands lifting me onto a stretcher. I couldn't get my eyelids open, so I didn't see the people who were lifting me, but I thought I might be hallucinating anyway because I heard Guidry's voice saying, "I don't *know* what happened! I just got here!"

The next thing I knew I was in a hospital

bed and a nurse was standing beside me adjusting a bag of fluid on an IV stand.

She saw me looking at her and said, "Hi. Everything's fine. You're back from surgery and your leg's going to be just fine."

Michael's worried face swam into view. Paco was beside him trying to smile but failing. There was Guidry again, too, and he didn't seem to be a hallucination.

Steven was also there, all ramrod straight and embarrassed. The other men stood on the opposite side of my bed from him, as if they had consigned him to the outer fringes of decency.

The nurse said, "On a scale of one to ten, how would you rate the pain in your leg right now?"

My leg hurt like a mother-effer.

I said, "Ten."

She put a call button in my hand. "Push this button whenever you feel pain, and it will release some morphine. Don't be stoic. Pain is not good. Don't be afraid you'll get too much morphine, either. The amount you can get in any given time is controlled, so make sure you stay ahead of the pain."

I pushed the button. In seconds, the pain lessened to a tolerable level.

I said, "I love you."

She laughed. "Okay, gentlemen, you can

have a few minutes with her, but *only* a few minutes."

She left the room, and Steven spoke.

"Ms. Hemingway, I apologize for this, but I have to ask you what happened."

"Lena ran at me when I got out of my car. She had a hypodermic needle in one hand and a knife in the other."

Suddenly alarmed, I looked at Michael and Paco. "Be careful around the driveway. That needle is on the ground. It probably has curare in it. Don't walk around barefoot until it's removed."

Paco said, "Dixie, the crime-scene people are there. They'll cover every inch of the place. They'll find it."

Of course they would. I felt stupid for not remembering that. I closed my eyes. My leg didn't hurt at all.

Steven said, "So Lena was running at you with a needle and a knife. Then what happened?"

I opened my eyes. "I had this branch in my hand, and it knocked the needle out of her hand."

"A branch?"

I closed my eyes. I was very sleepy. "It had fallen from the oak tree."

"Ms. Hemingway, try to stay with me, and I'll get out of your hair forever."

I opened my eyes. "Lena and I fought. I kicked at her knife, and she cut me. I knocked the knife out of her hand, and I got to it before she did, but she was choking me. Then Peter came and pulled her off me. He shot her in the head." To my total surprise, I began to sob. "Her head blew up, brains and bone all over the place."

Guidry leaped to hand me a tissue, and Michael said, "I think she's talked enough."

Steven said, "What about Briana?"

"Lena had already killed Briana before I got home. I guess they both thought I had a copy of the list in my apartment."

Steven said, "Did Peter kill Lena in self-defense?"

While I tried to get my brain to sift through all the implications of the question, Guidry said, "This is not a court of law. She's given you everything you need to know."

He said it in his homicide-detective voice, and Steven dipped his chin a fraction in silent acknowledgement of Guidry's knowledge and experience.

Steven said, "Okay, I'll leave you for now. I hope you have a speedy recovery."

He left without saying good-bye to the men in the room. They all watched him go with narrowed eyes showing their disdain for him. As far as they were concerned, he was responsible for my cut leg.

I felt a surge of alarm and tried to sit up, sending a current of pain to my foot.

"My pets! I have to get somebody to run with Billy Elliot and take care of the cats!"

Guidry said, "I've already taken care of that. While you were in surgery, I called all the owners and explained the situation. They all said they had backup plans, and for you not to worry. Tom Hale said that his girlfriend would run with Billy Elliot until you're back on the job."

"When will that be?"

They looked uncomfortable, Paco and Guidry turning to Michael to answer the question.

"The doc says you'll need about six weeks to recover. You'll be able to get around in a walking cast sooner than that, but you had a deep cut, and you have to give it time to heal."

I hit the morphine button and closed my eyes.

I heard Paco whisper something, and Michael spoke again.

"Okay, kid, Paco and I are going to go home now. Our place is swarming with cops, and Ella's probably freaking out. Don't worry about anything. Everything is going to work out great. We'll clean that stain on your porch, and when you come home everything will be absolutely normal. Including you."

He leaned close and kissed my forehead. "Love you, kid."

Paco did the same, adding a whispered, "Don't get amorous with Guidry in this bed. It's too narrow. You'd fall out and break your other foot."

I smiled weakly, but I didn't think anything would ever seem funny again.

I heard the door close, then heard Guidry drag a chair close to the bed.

With my eyes still closed, I said, "Where did you come from?"

"After we talked on the phone, I had a stroke of good sense and drove to the airport. Hopped the next flight out and got to SRQ before sunset. Rented a car and drove to your place expecting to surprise you. Instead, I found EMTs loading you into an ambulance, a couple of dead bodies, and Sergeant Owens Mirandizing a weeping guy in handcuffs. I grabbed your backpack from your Bronco, because I knew you kept your phone and your client records in it, and followed the ambulance to the hospital. I still don't know who all those dead people were, or what their connection was to you."

"It was Cupcake's cat."

"What?"

"Cupcake's cat took a paper that Briana dropped when she left a pair of Nikes on his bed, and everybody thought I found it."

"I shouldn't have asked you. Go to sleep."

"Why did you come?"

Even in my drugged state, I knew he took a long time to answer.

"We'll talk when you're awake."

My eyelids flew open. "I'm awake now."

Guidry eased his butt down on the side of the bed and took my hand. "I wanted to see you."

I came more alert. "Why now?"

He took a deep breath. "I wanted to make sure your decision not to come to New Orleans was final."

"You've met somebody."

"It's not serious."

"But it could become serious."

"I didn't want to tell you over the phone."

"Ethan Crane asked me out."

Guidry squeezed my hand. "We are who we are, Dixie."

I punched the morphine button and closed my eyes.

With my voice slurred and drowsy, I said, "I remember a novel set in India about a pair of star-crossed lovers. The woman in the story said, *We are peacock and tiger.* I guess we're like that, too."

"Are you saying I'm a peacock?"

I giggled. "Well, you're the one with the fancy clothes. Where do you get that stuff, anyway?"

"My older sister is the buyer for the men's department at Nordstrom's in Houston. She gives them to me."

"I hope she makes sure they're not fakes."

I drifted to sleep for a minute or an hour, and Guidry touched my shoulder.

"Dixie? I have to catch a flight back home. Are we okay?"

"You know what I'm scared of? I'm scared one day I'll want to be with you and you'll be settled down with some other woman and not want me."

He leaned down and kissed my forehead. "I'll always love you. Be happy."

He left the room, pulling the door closed behind him. I watched his broad back and felt tears slip down my face. But I did not call him back.

I hit the morphine button again and let drugs carry me into oblivion.

23

At Briana's memorial service, Cupcake pushed me in a wheelchair with a raised extension to hold my leg. It was a private ceremony that Cupcake had arranged and paid for. He and Jancey stood beside me near the open grave while a priest who had never met Briana mumbled words that might or might not have held meaning to her. There were no friends or family.

It was a brief service, with none of the melodrama that had attended Briana's life. Instead, a biodegradable urn holding her ashes was lowered into a hole, Cupcake shoveled dirt from a waiting mound on it, and we all tossed a rose on the dirt.

I hadn't liked Briana or respected her, but I admired her for overcoming deprivations I couldn't even imagine.

As Cupcake trundled me across the bumpy cemetery grounds, I caught a glimpse of Steven leaning on a tombstone across the way.

When we'd all got settled in Cupcake's car and were leaving the expanse of green grass interspersed by little white markers, Jancey said, "Cupcake, what will her marker say?"

"I told them to just put the name Briana Weiland and the date of her death. I don't know her birth date."

From my position stretched in the backseat, I said, "Do you think that was her real name?"

I saw Cupcake and Jancey exchange a look.

Cupcake said, "Her real name was Robbie Brasseaux."

I felt like an idiot. I should have figured that out for myself.

"When did you know?"

"It was the Nikes. It took me a while to get it, but Robbie was the only person in the world who would have brought me those Nikes."

My leg throbbed, and I wondered if I'd lost so much blood that I'd gone stupid.

I said, "But the Nikes were fakes."

"That was the whole point."

"I don't understand."

He looked at me in his rearview mirror and grinned, dimples flashing. "You're not supposed to. Robbie and I had a connection, I'm not sure what you'd call it, but we sort of saw things the same way, read the same things into movies and stories. I was a nut about Nikes, and Robbie teased me about it. When I took the money I got from robbing our first house and bought a pair of Nikes, it cracked Robbie up." His face went sober. "Robbie used his share to buy food."

"So —"

"So all these years later I come home and find a pair of Nikes in the middle of my bed. Nobody could have left them except my old white, skinny, redheaded friend Robbie Brasseaux, but Robbie hasn't been in my house. Instead, a famous model named Briana has been there, and Briana was white, skinny, and had red hair. Which made her a fake because she was really Robbie. And that's why Robbie left fake Nikes. It was a little joke he knew I'd get."

"Why didn't you tell Steven that Briana was Robbie?"

He took a deep breath. "I didn't figure it was any of his business. Besides, Robbie had enough trouble in his life without people knowing he'd gone and got himself turned into a woman."

Jancey nodded. She and Cupcake had apparently discussed the whole thing and she agreed with him that Briana's real identity was nobody's business.

I said, "Briana said she had killed her pedophile uncle when she was sixteen. She suspected that you had told a story about her hiding in the swamps that threw the police off while she ran away to New Orleans. Did you?"

A muscle worked in Cupcake's jaw. "Robbie didn't kill just his uncle, he killed his entire family. His drunken abusive uncle, his mean-as-a-wolverine aunt, and his three slack-jawed cousins who'd bragged about sodomizing him. Shot them while they slept. He did what he had to do to survive."

I didn't press him to tell me anything else.

Some loyalties are almost sacred. Some secrets are best left undisturbed.

The employees of Thorndike Press hope you have enjoyed this Large Print book. All our Thorndike, Wheeler, and Kennebec Large Print titles are designed for easy reading, and all our books are made to last. Other Thorndike Press Large Print books are available at your library, through selected bookstores, or directly from us.

For information about titles, please call:
(800) 223-1244

or visit our Web site at:
http://gale.cengage.com/thorndike

To share your comments, please write:

Publisher
Thorndike Press
10 Water St., Suite 310
Waterville, ME 04901